BOUND BY MY FATHER'S BEST FRIEND

CLUB RADIANT

EMILIA ROSE

CHAPTER
ONE

HEATHER

A WAFT of vanilla and hot, sweaty sex drifted through my nose as I took my first step into Radiant, a BDSM sex club in Pittsburgh that catered to the upper class. Half-naked women danced around shiny metal stripper poles, their breasts swaying in every which direction. Couples swapped an outrageous amount of spit on black suede couches in the back.

I glanced around nervously and continued into the club by myself. As far as I knew, not many BDSM newbies like me came here, except my bestie, Sierra. But I was only here for one thing tonight anyway.

To lose my virginity.

"Can I help you?" a waiter with devilish brown eyes said to my left. "You look lost."

Cheeks flushing, I snapped out of my thoughts and gave him a small smile. "I, um … I'm new here."

He chuckled. "I can see that. Anything I can help you find?"

"The owner."

The waiter's eyes widened. "The owner?"

"Yes," I said, scanning the club. "I have an arrangement with him tonight."

"Are you Miss Raquelle Chambers?"

"Yes."

No, that was just the fake name I had given the man I had been speaking to online for the past few weeks. I hadn't told him my real name, nor did he want to know it. I didn't know how many other women he had this kind of arrangement with, and I didn't care either. This was going to be a onetime thing, a one-night stand.

Lose my virginity, thank the man for his time, then get the hell out of here.

"Right this way," the waiter said, placing a platter of drinks down on the bar area and leading me toward the back of the club, where there were more private sections filled with CEOs and VIPs, who stared at me hungrily.

I pulled down my skirt as I walked around the booths of people and followed the waiter up a set of stairs and to some private rooms. My stomach was in knots, but I wanted to get this over with already. I didn't even want to exchange formalities.

We stopped in front of a large black door with the number four in a large golden numeral in the center.

The waiter leaned forward, placed his ear against the door, and knocked twice until someone called from inside, "Come in."

After giving me a small smile and the key to the room, the waiter left me on the second floor all by myself. I gnawed on the inside of my cheek, stepping closer to the door as a group of women dressed in lingerie stumbled out of the room next to me.

"Come on, Heather," I whispered to myself, fumbling with the key. "It's one night."

Just as I pushed the key into the knob, the door opened, and Hector Patton stared down at me through wide eyes. Hector Patton was a lot of things—like, apparently, the owner of the most popular BDSM club in the city, the sexiest fifty-six-year-old man I had laid my eyes on, a dominant playboy. But worst of all, he was my father's best friend.

And tonight, I would lose my virginity to him.

"Heather …" He paused, his gaze moving down my body for a moment longer than it should've—from my lips to my tits to my hips. He licked his lips and glanced back up at me. "What are you doing here?"

"You're the owner?" I whispered, heart pounding.

"One of them," he said, glancing down the hallway.

The group of women walked past my room, giggling and waving to Hector. And while I was just here to lose my virginity to him tonight, I couldn't help but feel the jealousy bubble up inside me. I'd never had a chance with a man more than twice my age, but … still …

"You didn't answer my question," he said.

After I finished glaring at the retreating women, I snapped my gaze back toward him and released my clenched jaw. This was it. Time to come clean and tell him that I was the one who had been chatting with him online, that I was the one who … had put up such a huge, bratty front with him for the past three weeks.

God, what had I gotten myself into? Hector was my father's best friend. He always saw right through me. As soon as I stepped into this room, he'd know that I had been lying online about knowing *anything* about BDSM.

"What. Are. You. Doing. Here?"

Heart pounding against my rib cage, I crossed my arms over my chest and grinded my thighs together. Was it bad that I kinda, sorta *liked* the tone of his voice? The demanding, dominant playboy that he had always been?

"Nothing," I found myself saying before I could stop.

A look of confusion washed over his face, and then finally, his eyes turned a shade darker. "Don't tell me that you're the woman I've been speaking with online."

Instead of saying anything, I pursed my lips together and shifted from foot to foot in the middle of the doorway. He stepped closer to me and wrapped one large hand around the front of my throat, forcing me to look up at him.

"You will answer me, Heather."

"And if I don't?"

I didn't know *what* I was getting myself into, but it seemed like I couldn't stop. I had come here for a reason, and I planned to go along with it. I wasn't backing away. I had waited *so long* to lose my virginity and couldn't wait any longer. All my friends always talked about how good it felt, and my vibrator wasn't doing it for me anymore.

Hector chuckled darkly and shook his head. "Fuck, I'm going to get myself into so much shit because of you."

Instead of pushing me away and telling me to get lost, he pulled me into the room, shut the door behind me, and then pressed my chest flush against it. I inhaled sharply, the feel of his dick against my ass making me hot in all the right places.

"You shouldn't be in a club like this," he said.

"Well, you shouldn't take peeks at me every chance you get," I said, again letting whatever the hell slip out of my mouth. But it was true. These past few weeks, I had caught him looking at me more than once during dinner with my father.

It wasn't one of those innocent looks either.

He tensed behind me, fingers strumming against the column of my throat. "Your father can never know."

CHAPTER
TWO

HEATHER

HECTOR GROWLED INTO MY EAR, his hand still around the front of my throat, "Do you understand me?"

My breath hitched. "What happens if I tell him?"

Instead of answering me, he pulled me off the door and thrust me against the large black bed in the center of the room. I landed on the mattress on my back, nipples pressing hard against my lacy bra.

"Take off your clothes," he said, pulling off his belt and stalking toward me.

Eyes widening slightly, I pressed my thighs together.

This was it. Tonight, I would lose my virginity to my father's best friend.

"Take them off," he said, voice harsher. "Now."

Hurriedly, I pulled off my shirt and shimmied out of my skirt until I sat in nothing but a skimpy lingerie set. For years, I had been aching for him to touch me. I had snuck longing glances at him one too many times.

After letting his shirt fall off his shoulders, he walked over to me and pushed me back onto the bed. He pulled off his pants, then his briefs, letting his hard cock hang between his legs. I sucked in a sharp breath.

Before I knew it, he had me lying back on the bed with his fingers buried between my legs. "You can breathe when you come," he growled into my ear, one hand over my mouth and nose and the other rubbing and smacking my clit. I whimpered into his hand, my legs trembling. "Don't take your fucking eyes off me."

I stared up at him, my breathing restricted and the pressure building quickly in my pussy. Warmth spread around my core, my skin becoming hot and needy. I spread my legs as wide as they could go to let him touch more of me.

"You're a needy little cumslut, aren't you?"

I nodded.

"Say it," he growled, still holding his hand over my mouth.

"I'm a needy little cumslut," I managed, the words muffled and driving me higher.

"Good girl," he said, moving his fingers faster against my clit. "Someone's learning."

My legs shot up into the air, spread wide. I arched my back and moaned out into his hand, my mind so fuzzy. Something about his degrading praise tipped me over the edge and pushed me into ecstasy.

It wasn't like anything that I'd felt before. It was better than my vibrator.

Hector pulled his hand away from my face, allowing me to breathe. I sucked in a deep breath, my little pussy pounding at the mere feel of his hands on my body still. He looked down at my pussy and continued to make small circles between my pussy lips.

"Please," I whispered, staring up at him and admiring how sinful he looked right now. This was wrong, so wrong. He was my father's best friend, yet I couldn't stop thinking about how he'd feel inside me. "I want you inside me, Hector. Please."

Hector slipped his fingers down my folds and thrust two inside me.

I whimpered and squirmed on the bed, brows furrowed together. "Not like that."

"How, Heather?"

He stared down at me, waiting for me to answer him, like I had always done online and over the phone. And while I was somewhat of a brat in real life, I had never begged for someone to put their cock inside me.

It sounded so wrong, so distasteful. And I was so nervous. So fucking nervous.

"How?" he repeated again, his voice stronger and more demanding.

"I want your dick inside my pussy," I said.

He grunted against me, as if he had been wanting to hear those words for years now, then crawled on top of me and between my legs, his fingers still buried deep inside my cunt. "Next time I have you," he said, pulling his fingers out and stuffing them into my mouth, "I'm going to tie you to this bed and refuse to let you leave all night."

When he brushed the head of his cock against my entrance, I whimpered. My toes curled, and I wrapped my legs around his waist to bring him down closer to me. He rubbed his cock between my pussy lips.

"Beg for it, Heather."

"Please."

He rubbed it against my clit.

"Oh God, please," I pleaded. "Please, put it—"

Before I could say another word, he thrust himself inside me, inch by inch. I curled my fingers into his shoulders and scrunched my brows together, a slight pain lingering in my core.

He shuddered against me. "You feel so fucking good."

I whimpered and buried my head into the crook of his neck, hoping that he wouldn't see the slight pain on my face. He felt so huge inside me, stretching out my walls and making me full with his cock—and hopefully his cum too.

His cum …

My pussy tightened around him, becoming wetter at the thought of him thrusting every inch of himself and every drop of his cum deep into me. Hector stilled in my pussy, then slowly pulled out.

"Your pussy is so tight, Heather," he grunted. "It's almost like you're a virgin."

Pressing my lips together, I decided not to answer him. Instead, I held on to him tightly and threw my head back, the pressure turning into pleasure and my tense body slowly relaxing in his arms. My brat had exited the room a long time ago, and I could do nothing, could say nothing, could think about nothing but him.

"More," I whispered, digging my nails into his shoulders. "Please."

He rested his head against mine and placed his lips at the corner of my mouth, leaving a lingering kiss as he thrust into me again. Unable to stop myself, I shifted my head and kissed him on the mouth. The moment that our lips touched, pleasure shot through my body.

Our lips moved together, faster and with more need. I was desperate for him. Aching for him.

"More," I mumbled into our kiss.

He thrust himself faster and faster into my tight pussy, pushing me closer to the edge each time. My lower body tensed, my clit aching as his hips pounded against me. I moaned into our kiss and came all over his cock.

"Please, come inside me," I whispered. "Please."

Hector grunted into my mouth, shoved his dick as deep as it could go, and came inside me. I rested against the mattress, pussy pulsing on every inch of his dick as he pulled it out of me. My chest heaved up and down, my mind like putty.

"Fuck," he mumbled, sitting back on the bed.

"Oh gosh," I whispered.

Suddenly, he tensed next to me. "There's blood," he said, brows furrowed down at his blood- and cum-covered dick. There was a moment, a single moment, of confusion that washed across his face. Then, realization hit him hard, and he finally glanced up at me through wide eyes. "Were you a virgin?"

I pulled the blankets over my naked body and shimmied out of the bed, turning away from him. It wasn't any of his concern if I had been a virgin or not. I had come to his BDSM club for a reason, and now, it was my time to leave.

Scrambling, I picked up my clothes. All I could do was repeat to myself over and over and over again that I needed to leave, that I couldn't stay, that this really was a onetime thing, and that Hector was nothing but bad news.

"You can't just walk away from me," he growled, like he owned me or something.

After pulling on my clothes, I hurried to the door. I didn't want to talk about being a virgin. I didn't want to even think about it. It was over, and it hadn't been as painful as all my friends had said it'd be.

"Watch me," I said.

He grabbed my wrist and pulled me toward him until our bodies collided. "Stop being a fucking brat for once, Heather. I know you get off on it, but this shit is serious." He paused. "You really haven't had sex before?"

"That's none of your business," I growled, ripping myself out of his hold and grabbing the door handle.

He placed his large hand on the door so I couldn't open it. "Yes, it is."

"And why?" I asked, crossing my arms and glaring at him. "What would've happened if you had known I was a virgin before this all started? You would've still asked me to come to your club, bent me over your bed, and fucked me senseless. It doesn't matter."

"Heather," he growled, jaw twitching, "you're my best fucking friend's daughter."

"Yeah," I said, shaking my head. "And you still fucked me. So, what does it matter?"

"It matters because, now, you're mine," he said harshly, pinning me against the door and taking my chin in his hand. "You're fucking mine, and you don't get to run off and away from me. You don't get to go back home and see that kid who is always all over you when I'm there."

"Archie," I corrected.

"I don't give a fuck what his name is, Heather." He slipped his knee between my thighs and pressed his cock against the side of my hip. "No other man gets to even *look* at you the way that I do. You knew what you were getting yourself into when you walked into my club."

"No, I—"

"Yes, you fucking did. I warned you not to come unless you were serious about *everything* that came with this kind of lifestyle, with me being the possessive and jealous asshole that I am."

I swallowed hard and stared up at him, wanting to bitch him out, but not knowing the first thing that I would say. Everything he had told me was true. He *had* warned me, and I had gotten off on the thought of someone being so obsessed with me that they wouldn't let another man look at me. I had never gotten that kind of attention before.

But we couldn't do this. Dad would find out.

He dipped his head and murmured into my ear, "You don't know how fucking long I've wanted you, how many women I've been with, imagining they were you. You leave my club without me tonight, and I will come and find you."

CHAPTER
THREE

HECTOR

FUCK, *what am I doing?*

I shoved my cum-covered cock back into my pants, zipped them up, and grabbed my tie hanging off the bedside. Heather had already pulled on her clothes, and while it wasn't like me to leave a woman without giving proper aftercare, I needed to breathe for a damn second.

Heather was my business partner's daughter, and she had been a virgin before I slept with her.

"Stay put," I said again so she wouldn't leave.

After slipping out the door, I headed straight for my office. I shouldn't have let that happen. But I loved putting brats into their places, and, God, did Heather love being a brat. She had always been one around her parents, and every damn time ... I had to hold myself back from bending her over my knee and spanking her straight in front of her father.

My dick stiffened *again* in my pants as I thought about how much she'd love that.

If he found out that I'd fucked her, everything that I had worked so hard for would be over.

"The hell are you going in such a rush?" Charlie, an adult-film actor, asked.

"I need a drink," I murmured.

"Bar is that way," Charlie said, nodding in the opposite direction.

After sighing, I stopped and glanced over the railing and down into the bar area, where people were dancing, drinking, and watching other members fuck in the next room. I ran a hand through my hair and cursed under my breath.

"What're you doing up here?" I asked.

A small smirk crossed his face. "Reserving a glass room."

"For?" I asked, arching a brow.

"If I shoot any more videos at my house, Athena is going to figure out what I do."

I leaned back against the railing and shoved a hand into my pocket. "I thought you had a thing for her?"

He tensed. "Who told you that?"

"You talk about her all the time."

"She's my best friend."

"Mmhmm."

"Plus, she doesn't like me like that." He glanced over my shoulder and toward the way I had come. "Anyway, I gotta get home. We're watching a movie tonight, and if I'm late again, she's going to ask questions."

As he headed down the hall, I shook my head and continued toward the offices.

Michelle, my adopted sister, walked down the hall toward me, black red-bottomed shoes clacking against the floor. I let out another audible sigh because I knew that I would be stopped yet again. Michelle loved talking our brother Steven's ear off. And when he wasn't around, she bothered me.

"Who's the girl?" Michelle hummed.

"What girl?"

"The girl who just snuck out of your room?"

"For fuck's sake," I mumbled, storming away from Michelle and back to the room.

Heather was gone.

A low growl escaped my throat, and I headed toward the bar.

If she left after I explicitly told her not to … if she slipped and told her father that she had come here tonight to meet someone, he would ask me about it. And I'd have to lie to him. After all the damn years we'd worked together.

"Heather!" I called over the music, scanning the crowd for any sight of her.

I searched the crowd. Once. Twice. Then a third time.

Nothing.

After sweeping the crowd for a fourth time, I grabbed my coat from the coatroom and yanked it over my shoulders. I gritted my teeth and stormed out into the cold. When I found that brat, I'd punish her for it.

CHAPTER
FOUR

HEATHER

"SIERRA!" I shouted, slamming open our door and rushing into the apartment.

I couldn't believe what had just happened, and I needed to tell someone. Anyone. Sierra and Athena were my two closest friends, but Athena didn't live with us. She was probably with Charlie for movie night again.

"What's going on?" Athena said from the couch, munching on a Clif Bar.

"What're you doing here?" I asked. "Where's Sierra?"

She giggled and stood. "Wow, rude much?"

"You know I didn't—"

"I know," she said with a smile. "I just finished my workout up at Trees Hall and wanted to shower before I headed all the way back to my place. I might or might not have let myself in right before Sierra left to go see some guy."

Ah, that was right. Sierra had gone down to Radiant tonight to meet a guy that she had been talking to for a while. Just like me … except he was her professor and she had already lost her virginity to him a couple of weeks ago.

After setting my belongings on the counter, I straightened out my clothes. "Well …"

Athena grabbed her water bottle on the counter, looking me up and down. "You look like you're glowing."

"I lost my virginity," I blurted.

"You what?" Athena asked.

"I lost my virginity," I said, heart racing inside my chest.

"To who?!"

A giggle escaped my mouth. "To maybe … an older man?"

"Like someone who's eighty?"

"No!" I exclaimed. "Who do you think I am?"

She snickered.

"Like somebody who's twice my age, not eighty. He's my father's best friend."

Mouth dropping open, she stared at me through wide eyes. "He's your what?!"

"Dang, Athena, do you need a hearing aid from all that music you blast during your workouts?" I playfully rolled my eyes at her, my cheeks becoming hotter by the second because it felt so sinful to repeat this out loud. "He's my father's best friend."

God, I couldn't get the way his hands were all over my body out of my mind. It was like his touch was burned into my skin, his mouth on my neck, his dick buried deep inside me. I wanted it to happen again. And again and again and again.

"Oh my God." Athena placed her hand on her chest. "We need all the details tomorrow."

"Tomorrow?" I repeated. "Where are you going?"

"It's movie night with Charlie."

Of course, but she couldn't leave me now! I needed someone to gush about all this to, and besides … if Hector was the type of Dom that he had portrayed in all those messages online, then he was probably on his way over to punish me.

And he wouldn't do anything with Athena here, right?

Besides, I *definitely* hadn't left to piss off Hector.

He had wanted me to stay put in some BDSM club that I had

only gone to so I could lose my virginity, and I didn't like being told what to do. I hated it. Especially because Mom and Dad tried to control my life enough.

Every single time that I was bratty in front of my parents, he looked at me like he wanted to put me in my place. Now, he could. And I had walked out of that club—run out of the club—like I wanted him to.

"Movie night again?" I hummed.

She smiled softly. "Yes."

"When are you going to finally admit that you love him?"

She rolled her eyes. "I do not love him. We're just friends."

"Friends who fuck?"

Suddenly, her eyes became even wider. "We do not."

I giggled. "But you want to."

After waving her hand dismissively at me, she walked to the door. "I'll see you later."

Before she could slip out the door, I jogged over and grabbed her wrist. "Please."

If she didn't stay, Hector would be over soon. Punishing me. And, hell, I didn't know if I would be ready for what he had in store for me. I was all talk, zero play until tonight in that sex club of his, lying on that bed ...

"I have to go," she said. "Charlie is waiting for me."

After shaking me off, she sent me a supportive smile and slipped out of the apartment. I sighed and shut the door after her, sulking back to the couch. I collapsed onto it, left alone with my thoughts and his cum buried deep in my pussy.

Moonlight and the light hum of cars on Fifth Avenue drifted through the apartment. I stared through the large windows and shook my head, still unable to believe what had actually happened tonight.

I'd lost my virginity tonight.

My fucking virginity.

To my father's best friend.

Since senior year of high school, I'd had the biggest goddamn crush on that man, though I never thought that I would actually have a chance with him. And yet the world had seemed to drop this right into my lap.

A few moments later, someone banged on the front door. I leaped up from the couch and walked over to the door, searching the kitchen for Athena's keys because if she was back so soon, it meant that she'd completely forgotten them.

"Don't tell me that you forgot your keys this time. You always do—"

Instead of Athena, Hector stood at my door with his brows furrowed in an angry stare and a rope in his hands.

CHAPTER
FIVE

HEATHER

"WHAT-WHAT ARE YOU DOING HERE?" I asked, backing up into the apartment.

Hector stalked into the room, shut the door behind him, and locked it, the thick black rope dangling from his hand and dragging against the floor with every step that he took toward me. "You know why I'm here."

After regaining from the shock of why he had rope, I cleared my throat. "No, I don't."

But I knew why he was here. I had run away from him when he told me not to.

"Don't fucking lie to me, Heather."

Inches from the couch, I rocked back on my heels, smiled sweetly at him, and pressed my pointer fingers together in an attempt to make myself look as shy as possible. Because shy girls like me weren't bratty. "I seriously don't know—"

"You ran away from me"—he snapped his hand around the front of my throat and forced me to look up at him through my lashes; his teeth were gritted together, his nostrils flaring in the way I had only seen them do when something went wrong in the business—"when I told you not to."

"I did no such thing," I hummed.

God, getting him angrier made the heat grow hotter between my legs.

"Don't fucking play with me, Heather."

I pressed my lips together from saying something stupid, but I couldn't help myself.

"Or what?" I asked.

Within a moment, Hector twirled me around, bent me over the couch, and began twisting the rope around my arms. I shoved my shoulder back against his to push him away, moved my body back and forth in an attempt to stop him, threw my leg back to kick him in the shin. But the binds only became tighter around my forearms until I couldn't move them.

"Let me out."

"If you had followed my directions," he said into my ear, "I was going to be easy on you."

"Fuck you—"

Before I could finish my sentence, he shoved four fingers into my mouth. I gagged on them, spit rolling down my chin, and glared back at him.

"Bratty girls like you don't get to talk back to their masters."

Warmth exploded between my thighs, my pussy clenching harder.

"Do you understand?" he growled.

I nodded to please him so I could answer his next question with a bratty answer.

After pulling his hand out of my mouth, he pulled me up by the binds and pushed me into the closest bedroom, which was thankfully mine and not Sierra's. Then, he slammed the door and shoved me down onto the bed.

"Why did you leave?"

"Because I only wanted you to take my virginity. And besides, I had another guy comin—"

He snatched my chin. "Stop being a fucking brat, Heather. It's pissing me off."

"Good. Maybe you'll—"

"Maybe I'll shove my cock down your throat and give you your first punishment."

"You won't—" My sentence lodged itself in my throat as he shoved me from the bed to my knees in front of him and unzipped his jeans, his cock springing out of them. I stared up at him through wide eyes, never having done something like this before.

Twenty-four goddamn years of my life, and I hadn't even given a blow job.

"Open your mouth and be a good girl for me. This doesn't have to be hard."

I pressed my lips together and stared up at him.

"Don't force me to do this," he warned. "You won't like it."

Still, I stared up at him and didn't open my mouth.

He drew his tongue across the front of his teeth, a dark chuckle leaving his throat. "Oh, I am going to fucking ruin you," he growled as his forefinger and thumb pinched my nostrils shut, so I really couldn't breathe.

But I wasn't going to give up that easily.

Tears slowly began filling my eyes, my cheeks growing hotter by the second.

No way was I going to give in to him. He'd break before I … before I …

"Getting hard to breathe, isn't it, *brat*?"

I shook my head, but I was starting to see stars.

"Any second now," he taunted, "you're going to give in to me."

Heat coursed through my body, and I finally opened my mouth wide to suck in a huge breath in an attempt to do it before he could slip inside of me. But the second I opened my mouth, he was already inside me, hitting the back of my throat and making me gag.

Digging my nails into my palms, I glared up at him through teary eyes and pulled back. But his hands were around the back of my head, holding me in place so I couldn't move. And with my arms tied behind my back … he had full control.

His gaze was dark, eyes hooded. He shoved as much of his dick into my mouth as he could, and when I couldn't take any more, he stepped closer to me in order to force another inch or two. The light from the buildings surrounding us flooded in through the large windows, hitting the side of his perfectly sculpted face.

"I'm in control, Heather. Not you."

"Fuck you," I gargled on his dick, still gagging.

"We're going to train this bratty little mouth of yours until you learn not to talk back."

That would never happen, but he could try.

A moment later, in the middle of my gagging and spitting fit, his phone buzzed in his jeans pocket on the floor. He peered down at it, then back at me, and then he pinched my nose closed again. "Pick it up for me and answer it."

My eyes widened.

"Now."

I reached down into his jeans and pulled out his phone, pressing the green button—or at least I hoped it was the green button, but it was hard to tell through my teary gaze. Why was he doing this now?! In the middle of—

"Hey, Hector," my dad said through the speaker.

Gagging softly, I stared at the phone in complete horror.

While I expected Hector to shut it off immediately, that asshole moved it even closer to my mouth, so if I said a word, if I moaned or choked or gagged on him, Dad would hear it. He'd fucking hear it, and I would be humiliated for the rest of my life.

"Something happen at the office?" Hector asked.

"I wanted to talk to you about the finances for Q4. Are you busy?"

He shoved another inch of himself inside me. "A bit, but I can talk."

Sputtering on his cock, I held back an audible gag and swallowed the spit that had pooled in my mouth. Tears streamed down my face, my cheeks hot and the need to breathe growing stronger and stronger with every passing second.

Except Hector didn't care.

Those cold, dark eyes met my glossy gaze as he talked on the phone with my father for who knew how long. He laced one hand into my hair and moved my head back and forth on his dick until my throat was sore and the ropes were digging into my wrists.

"We should move her position," Dad said. "I was thinking under you."

Move Evelyn under Hector?

I had only been gathering pieces of the conversation, but if that meant what I thought it meant, then Evelyn would be working even more closely with Hector, and she was the prettiest —and smartest—woman at their company.

Jealousy swirled inside me, and I found myself bobbing my head back and forth on his dick without him having to force me to do it himself. I stared up at him through stinging eyes, desperate to make an unforgettable impression on him.

Though I still wasn't sure if he liked this. He was giving nothing away.

"Fuck," he murmured, quiet enough so Dad couldn't hear. "Good girl."

"What do you think?" Dad said over the phone.

I sat on my knees in front of Hector, his cock buried down my throat and my tongue flicking against the inches that I couldn't reach. Hector tilted his head back, eyes rolling, and grasped one of my tits in his large, rough hand.

"That's great," he murmured, his cum shooting down my throat. "That's *fucking* great."

"Good. We can talk more about it tomorrow." Dad paused. "You sound busy."

Hector cleared his throat and took the phone from me. "Talk tomorrow."

After Hector pressed the End Call button, he pulled out of me. I fell forward onto my rug , shoulder first, and swallowed what I could have his cum and my spit. My chest rose and fell quickly, my mind numb.

While I expected Hector to growl at me and tell me that he was leaving, that I should've learned from this punishment, he picked me up and gently set me on the bed. After sitting behind me, he unraveled the rope and tossed it onto the floor beside me. He took my hand in his and then suddenly placed his lips on the indents on my wrists from the rope.

What the hell was that?

"For once in your life, listen to me and stay here." Hector pulled on his jeans. "I'll get you water."

As he left the room, I stared with wide eyes at the door, surprised that he was being so nice to me after I had been nothing but a bratty little bitch to him. But the intensity quickly faded, and I didn't think I had it in me to be difficult anymore tonight.

Though still … jealousy reeled inside me at the thought of Evelyn getting closer to Hector. Because Hector might not know it, but he was mine. All mine. And nobody was going to get in the way.

CHAPTER
SIX

HECTOR

SITTING at my desk that overlooked Pittsburgh, I stared out the window and blew out a long breath. I hadn't been able to look Jacob, Heather's father, in his eye all day, and if I didn't start soon, he'd begin to notice.

What I had done was wrong. So, so wrong.

His daughter, who he trusted me with, was now mine. I had taken her virginity.

Without mercy.

I didn't care about the consequences. All I cared about was being with her, punishing her, making her mine after all these goddamn years that she had teased me, taunted me, tormented me with those not-so-innocent glances.

Someone knocked on my door, and I glanced up to see Jacob with Evelyn, file in hand.

Evelyn waved the file at me. "We picked these up from the financial department—Q4 documents."

Jacob released a sigh. "We should talk about them."

Fuck. "What is it this time?"

After they both sat in front of my desk, I kept my gaze on the file that Evelyn held against her chest. I couldn't believe what I had done not once, but twice last night. Heather knew exactly what she was fucking doing with being a brat.

It was hard for me to believe that she actually had been a virgin.

"Are you okay?" Jacob asked.

"I'm fine," I said quickly, pulling my gaze away. "Just stressed."

Because I fucked your daughter, and now, I can't get enough of her.

"What's up?" he asked.

We had been friends for so long that he knew exactly when something was wrong, when I was stressed about something other than work. I confided in him with everything. But this … this was off the table. What would happen when he found out what I had done to his daughter?

My pants tightened around my crotch, and I thanked the god that I didn't fucking believe in that I had been sitting behind my desk.

It wasn't like Heather hadn't wanted it. We'd talked online for so long. She marched right into my club. And she didn't leave when she found out who I really was.

But hell, neither had I.

"Do you want to talk about it?" he asked.

I let out another long breath and ran a hand over my face. "No, I'm good."

"You know you can tell me anything."

I bit back a chuckle because, no, I couldn't.

I nodded to the folder. "What's this report about?"

Evelyn handed me the folder.

"Just some numbers for the past year. The company has grown about twenty-four percent since last quarter, mainly because of Evelyn's efforts. Nothing bad." He chuckled. "I just like to get you riled up sometimes."

I rolled my eyes because he had done this since we'd started the company five years ago, and I should've known better. But I couldn't think straight. All day, I had been thinking about her. Nobody and nothing else but her.

The way she'd stared up at me last night. How much control she had given me … or more like how much I had taken from her. And how much possessiveness had crossed her face right before I was about to come.

"Great job, Evelyn," I offered.

I honestly didn't really like her, and I didn't want her working under me. Hell, I didn't need to babysit anyone else. She was one of our employee's daughters who was studying business, intelligent and nothing more than an intern who had been with us for almost a year now. Plus, I thought Jacob had a thing for her.

My phone buzzed on the desk, and I tilted it an inch toward me to see the notification.

But my facial recognition immediately unlocked the phone, and a message from Heather appeared on the screen. And it wasn't just a normal message from my best friend's daughter, but a fucking nude with the caption, **Bet you can't guess what I'm doing without your permission.**

Pants tightening even more, I immediately turned off the phone and slid it into my pocket. I glanced over at Jacob, who didn't even realize that his own innocent daughter's nude would be plastered on my screen if I were to open it again.

She was going to get me in so much fucking trouble.

But she was not getting away with that.

No fucking way.

Her bratty ass hadn't learned last night when I put her in her place. But one of these days … she'd learn. I didn't care what it took. I didn't care how long I had to tie her up. I didn't care how many times I would force her to come over and over and over again. She might be crying by the end of tonight, but she would learn.

I wasn't gonna let her get away with this.

For the first eighteen years of my life, someone else had had control. Someone else had beaten me or scarred me, locked me on a chain out in the rain with dogs bred to fight. And now that I had control … I wanted all of it.

Especially with her.

"By the way"—Evelyn cleared her throat—"I'm happy to work underneath you."

"Yes, me too," I lied. "Make sure you're in the office by six every morning."

"Yes, *sir*."

"Address me by Hector," I clarified, glancing down at my phone.

Because Sir and Master were reserved for someone else.

Someone who would learn the meaning of those words tonight.

CHAPTER
SEVEN

"THEY TOTALLY FUCKED." Sierra giggled at me, gaze lingering on Athena at the counter of Carnegie Coffee Company.

Athena hadn't messaged us back since last night, and this'd only solidified that the running joke that she and Charlie were hooking up was true.

Athena grabbed her Ashley's Egg Sandwich from the counter and walked over to us, her skin glowing and a huge smile on her face. She slowed down her pace, noticing Sierra's wicked expression, and then eventually stopped. "What?"

"Is he good?" Sierra asked, wiggling her brows.

"Is who good?"

"Charlie."

After an exaggerated eye roll, Athena sat next to me and grabbed her sandwich. "If we ever get together—and we will *not* because we're strictly friends—you will be the first ones to know about it, okay?"

"Somehow"—Sierra tapped her chin—"I feel like that's a lie."

"Come on," Athena hummed. "You think I'd be able to keep it to myself? Heather couldn't."

Sierra snapped her gaze to me, eyes wide. "You what?"

With my phone in hand, impatiently waiting for Hector to text me back, I pressed my lips together, cheeks burning. "Oh, well, I might or might not have hooked up with my father's best friend last night and—"

Sierra slammed her hands against the table and stood. "And you didn't tell me?!"

"Well, *you* were with Professor Big Dick last night."

Athena smirked as if she was enjoying the drama. "Heather is hooking up with her father's best friend. Sierra's sleeping with her sex ed professor. And it's always *me* who is the topic of everyone's slutty conversations."

"Because it's obvious that you and Charlie are fucking," someone said behind us.

Sun-Hee, Sun for short, walked up to our table and dumped her backpack beside Sierra. She was the fourth in our friend group and had been in Pittsburgh with us since undergrad. Back then, we'd shared a four-girl dorm room.

While Sun grabbed some coffee from the counter, I slouched down in my seat and opened my messages to Hector. I had sent him some spicy ones earlier today while he was at work and I was relaxing back in my apartment.

It had been weeks since I'd last had an afternoon to myself because I had been studying nonstop for Professor Eric's exam about the tech side of business—I honestly still couldn't wrap my mind around that course—and toying with Hector while he was at work with my father had seemed like the perfect way to pass time.

Me: Whoops ... these were supposed to go to someone else. xx

My lips curled into a smirk at the thought of him reading my messages and getting so pissed off at my brattiness. He had made it clear last night that he loved putting me in my place, loved fucking the brat right out of me.

Hector: Where are you?

Me: Why don't you come find me? <3

Hector: I'm not playing with you, Heather. Where the fuck are you?

I ground my legs together underneath the table, heat coursing through my body.

Me: What are you going to do when you find me?

Hector: Nothing that you'll enjoy.

Me: Hmm … I doubt that. I quite enjoyed last night. xx

Hector: I was going easy on you last night.

Me: Suuuure.

Hector: You wouldn't be able to handle a real punishment, Heather. You'd be fucking begging me to stop. Crying. Fucking sobbing. But I wouldn't because you are incapable of learning in other ways.

While Hector might've thought that was a punishment, my nipples hardened underneath my shirt, and I couldn't help the way my pussy clenched over and over. My thong was soaked through already, and I hadn't even seen him today.

Hector: If you make me find you, it'll be worse.

Me: I'm shaking in my boots.

My phone immediately began buzzing in my hand, his name on the screen.

I clicked the Ignore button. Then, three typing bubbles appeared on the screen.

To be an extra-spicy bitch tonight, I switched off his message and spotted one from my brother, Aaron. We were taking the same business class this semester, except he was an undergrad and Dad's favorite, and I was in grad school and hated what I was studying.

Aaron: Grades are posted.

Nerves built in my stomach, and I headed to my email.

This was the second time I was taking this class, and I had studied so, so hard.

A single email from my professor.

Heather,

I'm disappointed in your effort so far this semester. See me next class to talk about your failing grade on the most recent test. If you are actually studying the material, you should be doing better than this. Don't want it to get out to your father that you failed again.

Prof. Eric

Lips quivering, I bit down on my cheek to stop myself from sobbing out loud. I had studied for weeks for this exam and told Hector that I couldn't meet him until last night because my nights were taken up, trying to learn the material.

Material that wasn't even relevant to my degree.

And if I didn't pass this semester, then I would have to retake it *again* with Professor Eric and have to listen to these grueling remarks from not only him, but my father as well. How he wasn't going to pay if I couldn't pass. How this should be easy because it had been for him.

Another text from Hector lit up my phone, but I shut it off and stared at my computer.

What was I going to do?

Tears built in my eyes, and I … I let one fall.

Because Dad was right. I was nothing more than a mess.

CHAPTER
EIGHT

HECTOR

GRINDING MY TEETH TOGETHER, I stormed out of my office at Radiant. I had searched all over Pittsburgh tonight just to find Heather. I had gone to her apartment, made it past the security guard, and banged on her door multiple times. Only for no response.

None.

She was taunting me, and she knew it.

"Where the fuck is she?" I growled underneath my breath, heading for Michelle's office.

She hadn't answered any of my calls or texts either.

"Have you seen Heather?" I asked Michelle, walking into her room without a knock.

"Who?" she asked, glancing up from the pile of Plaything Co. sex toys on her desk.

"The girl I was with yesterday. Has she returned?"

A small smirk crossed her face. "Why? Do you like her?"

"You're so annoying," I snapped, storming out of her office and down the hallway toward the coatroom. I didn't know how Steven put up with her bullshit any of the time because I tried to stay away from her as much as I could.

But running a business together made that hard.

After I shrugged on my coat, I headed straight for the front exit. I wasn't going to wait around here while Heather did God knew fucking what with God knew fucking who. She had made that comment yesterday that all she wanted to do was lose her virginity to me.

But I wasn't letting her off that easily. Wasn't going to let another man fuck her.

Screw that. She was mine.

Bracing myself for the fall chill, I shoved my shoulder into the door and bumped into Heather heading into Radiant. With her arms crossed over her chest and her head down, she muttered an apology and continued through the door.

Before she could get anywhere, I snatched her chin and forced her to look up at me. "Where have you been—"

Tears.

She stared up at me through glossy eyes, her chin wrinkled, as if she had been just crying or trying to hold herself together. My eyes widened, and I loosened my grip on her chin, gently tilting her face so I could see it better in the light.

"What happened?" I asked.

"Nothing."

"Don't bullshit me, Heather."

After gritting her teeth at me, she shoved my hand away. "I said, nothing happened."

"Who did this to you?" I growled, anger rushing through me.

"Nobody did anything, Hector!" she exclaimed. "I'm here to fuck you, then leave."

Nostrils flaring—because nobody ever wanted to just fuck and most wanted me for the money Steven, Michelle, and I had inherited from our parents—I snapped my hand around her wrist and pulled her inside Radiant to get out of the cold.

"Get off me," she growled, shoving me away again.

And while, any other time, I would've pinned her to the wall and forced her bratty mouth to apologize, I couldn't quite get into the headspace. She had been crying and wouldn't tell me why. She'd straight-up refused that it had even happened.

"You have fucking tears in your eyes," I said. "What happened?"

While I'd loved those tears last night, I was fuming at the thought of them now.

"Maybe someone face-fucked me as hard as you had last night," she snarled. "Drop it. Why do you even care?"

Why do I care?

"I'm not going to drop it, Heather," I said, ignoring her question. "And I'm not fucking you again unless you tell me what's going on."

She glared up at me through teary eyes, her stare becoming angrier and angrier by the second. And then, all of a sudden, her bottom lip quivered, and she burst out into tears. She slammed the side of her fist against my chest. "Why not?"

"Because you're a mess."

After her eyes widened, the tears spilling out of them, she twirled around and marched back toward the exit. "All I wanted was to relax, and you have to be an asshole," she gritted out. "I'll be a mess elsewhere with someone else."

Before she could slip out that door, I grabbed her wrist again. Yet instead of letting me pull her into the club, she continued to march right out the door and onto the sidewalk in the middle of the freezing fall breeze.

"Get off me," she said, but made no move to push me away. "I'm going home."

"No."

"What do you mean, no?" she asked. "You don't get to make decisions for me."

"I do when I know that you won't be able to drive home straight."

If she left like this and got into a car accident, Jacob would never forgive me.

At least, that was what I told myself … that this was all because of my relationship with Heather's father and not because she had done something to me last night. Not because I had always looked forward to business dinners with Jacob's family just so I could see her. Not because I'd only really ended up attending Jacob's family's Christmas parties for her.

"Have you eaten dinner yet?" I asked, continuing forward to my car parked on the side.

"No."

I glanced back at her. "Heather, it's almost ten."

"Yeah, well … I haven't had time."

"What've you been doing?"

"Crying. Now, will you get off me so I can go home?"

She dug her heels into the ground, so I released her wrist and turned around to face her.

"You're coming with me so I can make you dinner. And you're not going to whine about it."

The brattiness suddenly stopped, and she furrowed her brows. "You're going to make me dinner?" she repeated, almost surprised.

"Yes." I held out my hand for her to take. "Now, come with me."

I waited and I waited and I waited. And then she finally placed her hand in mine.

"Fine, but only because I'm hungry. Then, I'm going home."

"Sure."

But she wasn't going to leave without telling me who had made her cry.

I would make sure of it.

CHAPTER
NINE

THIRTY MINUTES LATER, I sat at Hector's dining room table with a plate of warm pasta in front of me. I kicked my legs back and forth underneath my seat and took another bite of some of the best food I had ever eaten.

"I didn't know that you could cook," I hummed.

"You like it?"

A small smile crossed my lips, and I shrugged nonchalantly. "It's *okay*," I said—because that man had a huge ego and I was attempting to bring him back down to reality.

After rolling his eyes, he set his fork on his plate and wiped his mouth with a napkin. "Are you going to tell me why you were crying?"

"I've just had a bad day."

"What happened?"

I blew out a sigh. He wasn't going to let this go, was he?

"You're going to think it's stupid," I murmured, pushing spaghetti around on the plate before taking a scoop of it on my fork. "So, no, I don't want to talk about it, and I don't want to tell you. You'll judge me too."

"Did your friends judge you?"

"No, but—"

"Then, who did?"

After setting my fork back down on the plate, I crossed my arms. "My dad will."

He arched a brow. "Jacob will for what? He brags about you all the time."

I pressed my lips together to stop my chin from quivering. "If I tell you, will you drop it?"

"Yes."

Though something told me that he really wouldn't be dropping anything.

"Do you remember when we were talking online and planning to meet up for the first time, but I told you that I couldn't because I was studying for a test last week? Well, I failed it. See? Stupid. Now if you'd let me, I'd like to go back to eating in peace."

When I grabbed my fork again, that man's gaze burned into me.

I looked up at him. "What?"

"Why'd you fail?"

"Because I'm stupid," I said. "Now—"

"You're not stupid," he said. "Bratty? Yes. But not stupid."

My eyes lingered on him for a moment longer than they should've, a warm feeling spreading throughout my chest. I didn't know why I felt this way around him, why I had even agreed to come over or tell him any of this.

But nobody had ... said that to me before.

Every time I put myself down—except in front of my friends—nobody would ever say otherwise. Compared to Aaron, I felt like a complete idiot who couldn't do anything right. Hell, he was even starting his own company and had gotten over a million dollars in funding for it in undergrad.

Undergrad!

I was almost halfway through my twenties and couldn't pass a class.

"Yes, I am," I whispered.

Hector leaned across the table, took my chin in his hand, and tilted my head to look up at him. "No, you're not, Heather. Now, why did you fail? Did you not understand the material, or had I been keeping you up too late with my messages?"

My lips quivered again, the tears threatening to spill down my cheeks. I didn't want to cry in front of him again because it'd make me feel even more like an idiot, but I almost couldn't help it. He was usually so rough, but his touch right now ... was so gentle.

"I don't understand it," I whispered, a tear running down my cheek. "I've tried to."

"What is it?" he asked.

"The MBA program forces everyone to take a software development course," I said.

It had absolutely nothing to do with my track or what I actually wanted to do, so I thought it was so stupid that I had to learn how to code. But I couldn't back out of it now. I had gone through four years of undergrad and now nearly two years of grad school.

"Coding, huh?" he hummed.

"Yeah, but it's so hard."

"Do you want me to help you?"

I glanced up at him. "You know how to code?"

"I've picked it up along the way. My brother built a software company, so I know a bit."

But his smirk told me that he was selling himself short.

"You know more than just a bit, don't you?" I asked, narrowing my eyes.

His smirk widened even more. "I'll make learning fun for you."

"And how're you going to do that?" I asked, arching a brow.

"I have my ways."

CHAPTER
TEN

HEATHER

STUPID PROFESSOR ERIC.

With a balled fist, I stood in front of his door and pounded on it, pissed off that he'd made me embarrass myself in front of Hector last night. Usually, I tried not to let my emotions get the best of me, but I couldn't help it.

"Who is it?" Eric called from the other side of the door.

I resisted the urge to give the door my middle finger. "It's Heather."

While Hector had told me that he'd help me study for this stupid computer science software development class or whatever the hell it was, I still wanted to know what I had done wrong on the exam. Eric had even let us use the internet to simulate what real life coding was like.

And part of me was beginning to think that I hadn't failed because of my abilities.

But because Eric had something against me.

A couple moments later, Eric opened the door and stared down at me, his brown brows drawn together and his lips set in an angry scowl. "What are you doing here? My office hours ended twenty minutes ago."

"Why did you fail me?" I asked, walking right into his office.

I didn't care if his office hours had ended *two hours* ago. I had told him that I would be here now because I had class during his office hours and he wouldn't make time out of his schedule for me. Because he fucking hated me.

"Because you didn't study."

"I studied for the past week, nonstop, for this exam," I said, clenching my fists.

How dare he say that I hadn't studied, that I hadn't tried so damn hard for this exam! He didn't know anything about me, nor about how much I was actually trying to understand this material. I didn't even know why this was important.

"There is something you could do to pass," he suggested.

I glared over my shoulder, lip curled in disgust. If he was about to say what I thought he was going to say, I would report him to the dean of students and walk out of here with an A for it.

"You're disgusting," I snarled.

"It's not that," he said, eyes narrowed. "You're not attractive enough for me to lose my job over."

While it shouldn't have bothered me because that was sick of any teacher or professor to do, I couldn't stop my chest from tightening and my lips curling down into a frown. Because he had flat-out told me that I wasn't attractive.

I was pretty, but not as pretty as Evelyn was from Hector and Dad's company.

But come on; how unprofessional was that to say to his student?!

"Get me an interview at your father's company," he said.

"No."

"Then, you'll fail again."

"What?!" I exclaimed. "Why?!"

"Don't ask questions," Eric said. "I want an interview *and* a job."

Still recovering from the shit he had just said to my face, I pressed my lips together and walked out of his office. If he thought I was going to cheat my way through class, then he had another thing coming. If he failed me again, then I'd report him to the dean for bribing.

Because fuck him.

He deserved to be run over by a car multiple times.

Mumbling curse words under my breath, I stomped out of the building and headed to my car parked a couple of blocks down. Wind seared my face, making it even more difficult to walk in the dark. Once I reached my car, I slammed the door shut and blasted the heat.

Fuck Eric.

In a stressed and pissed-off mess—because of Professor Prick —I furiously drove to Radiant. I had told Hector that I'd be there at eight, and my car clock read 8:14. But he'd understand, right?

Or maybe he'd punish me for it.

Warmth gushed between my thighs, and I used it to forget about Eric.

All I wanted was Hector to use me, to help me forget about my grade, about how much I didn't really want to finish this business degree, and about the pressure that Dad constantly put on me to live up to the legacy my *younger* brother was already leaving.

Once I found an open parking spot, I parked on the side of the road and hurried through the chilly winds to Radiant. One of the reasons that I liked being a brat, especially for Hector, was that I didn't have to care so much about what he thought about me.

I didn't have to care about my grades, nor what a mess my life was turning out to be. I pushed through the first set of blacked-out doors, past Radiant security. I could do what I wanted and get pleasure from it.

When I pushed open the second set of doors, I bumped into someone.

"Oh, sorry," a woman said, walking toward the exit with a collar on her neck.

My eyes widened.

Evelyn.

The woman who was supposed to be working under Hector. The woman who I would never ever compare to in terms of looks and in business. The woman who was now at Radiant, where Hector was supposed to be tonight.

Evelyn widened her eyes at me, her cheeks flushed red.

What is she doing here?!

She opened her mouth, then shut it. Once. Then twice. Then, she hurried out of the building. I stared after her, eyes filling with tears because I couldn't think straight or logically at this point. Professor Prick had already gotten so deep into my head with that stupid, snide comment. Now, one of the prettiest girls was walking out of Radiant.

The BDSM sex club that Hector owned.

So, I did the only logical thing I could think of and walked out too.

CHAPTER
ELEVEN

HECTOR

WITH MY TEETH CLENCHED, I glared out my office window and down at Pittsburgh.

Where the hell is Heather?

She had told me that she'd be at Radiant at eight last night. Except eight came and went, then nine came and went, and then it was suddenly midnight, and she hadn't shown her face once. Hadn't answered my calls or my texts.

Buses stopped at the corner down on the street below and picked up passengers. I stood up and walked closer to the window, my hands balled into fists and stuffed deep into my pockets.

This morning, I had been nervous that something had happened to her, but then I'd heard Jacob talking on the phone with her during lunch. Less than a fucking hour ago! She had to have seen my messages and was intentionally ignoring them.

A low growl escaped my throat.

Acting like her usual bratty self.

"Mr. Patton?" Evelyn cleared her throat from my desk, sitting in one of the seats and glancing up at me over one of the files. She anxiously bounced her foot up and down. "What do you think?"

I ran a hand over my face and headed back to my desk, completely forgetting that she was here to review financial information with me that we'd received from the finance team this morning.

Low hums drifted through the room, and I glanced toward the vent. "Do you hear that?"

After clearing her throat and crossing her legs, she placed the file on my desk. "No."

Once I grabbed it from her, I leaned back in my seat and flipped through it. My phone sat on my desk, face up with a black screen. It was almost the end of the day, and I still hadn't received any messages from Heather yet.

"What do you think?" Evelyn continued. "I've created a plan for us to—"

Someone knocked on the door, and then Jacob walked into the room, gaze on Evelyn. Her cheeks tinted red, and she pressed her thighs together even harder. I arched a brow at them, then lifted my gaze to Heather.

Dressed in a short white tennis skirt and a high ponytail, she followed Jacob into my office. I turned back toward the window and cursed underneath my breath.

What is she doing here?! Teasing me. Taunting me. Thinking I won't make a move.

"Evelyn," Jacob said. "Working hard?"

Yet I couldn't care less about what was going on between Jacob and Evelyn.

"Good afternoon, Heather," I hummed, watching her closely.

"Mr. Patton," Heather sneered, not looking up at me once.

No Sir. No Hector. Just Mr. Patton.

A brat. A fucking brat.

I drew my tongue across the front of my teeth. "What are you doing here?"

I'm going to fucking punish her. So hard until she's crying those pretty tears.

For the first time today, she lifted her gaze to me. "Helping my father."

Jacob placed his hand over his right pocket, then his left. "Give me a second before our meeting. I left my book in my office."

Unlike usual, Evelyn didn't follow after him when he slipped out the door. She stayed glued to the spot, the hum of the AC drifting even louder through the room. I walked around my desk as Heather shuffled some papers together on a side table.

Not giving a fuck about what Evelyn thought, I grabbed Heather's ponytail and pulled back on it so she'd stare up at me with those huge fuck-me eyes. "If you think I won't punish you while your father's here, you're wrong," I whispered to her.

"Evelyn is—"

"Do you understand me?" I asked quietly.

She pressed her lips together and stared up at me, her ass pressed against the front of my pants. Instead of nodding like a good girl, she arched her back and moved her ass against my bulge, my dick throbbing.

"Hector, you—"

I tugged harder on her ponytail. "You are to address me as Sir."

Heather sucked in a breath, nervous eyes glancing from me to the door. "Sir."

Fuck…

She was too nervous to be a brat when Evelyn was in the room, and hearing her be a good girl, being able to tame her right here, made my dick throb. I pressed myself against her ass harder, wanting her to feel how *happy* it made me that she wasn't being a brat for once, wanting her to know that if she dropped the disrespectful attitude, I'd always be this hard for her.

The door opened behind me, and I released Heather's hair and stepped away from her before Jacob could see my body pressed against hers. He couldn't find out about us, but I wasn't about to let Heather be a brat around here.

Not when she was purposefully doing it because it'd piss me off.

While she still didn't look at me, her lips curled into a small smirk, and she sauntered toward her father, skirt bouncing every time she took a step, giving me a glimpse of her ass that I'd have red with handprints by the end of the night.

This was my company. Not hers.

I had the control here.

Forty minutes later, after we went through all the financials—though I couldn't focus because Heather kept playing footsie with me underneath my desk—Jacob stood and tapped Evelyn's shoulder. "I have a meeting with a couple of others that I'd like you to attend."

"I'll come with you," Heather said, smirking my way.

"Actually"—I cleared my throat—"if you don't mind, Jacob, I could use Heather's help."

Halfway to the door, Jacob nodded. "This is a private meeting, Heather. Why don't you help out Hector?"

"B-but—"

I stood up and followed them to the door. "Have a good one."

When Jacob walked out of the room with Evelyn for good, I twirled Heather around and pushed her against one of the bookcases. Breasts pressed against the books, she sucked in a sharp breath.

"You get one chance," I growled into her ear, loosening my tie. "Where were you last night?"

Instead of answering me, she threw her elbow into my ribs. I caught her elbow, yanked off my tie, and tied her arms behind her back so she couldn't elbow me, so she couldn't hit me, so she knew who was in control.

"My dad is going to walk in on us," she said. "Let me go."

A low chuckle escaped my throat, and I popped off one of her shirt buttons. "Let him walk back in then, Heather. I'll teach him how brats like you need to be punished so they learn. Because he's done a shit job teaching you respect, you're going to learn respect from a master."

CHAPTER
TWELVE

HEATHER

HECTOR bent me over his desk and sank his hand between my legs from behind, pushing his hand up my tennis skirt and cupping my wet pussy. "Of course, a dirty little slut like you isn't wearing any panties to come see me."

"I'm not here to see you," I gritted out.

"Bullshit," he growled. "We both know you're only here to tease me."

My nipples hardened against his desk, my pussy clenching. *Fuck.*

While one of his hands popped off my shirt buttons, he pushed one finger into my entrance. I clenched hard and bit back a whimper, not wanting to give him the satisfaction of making me feel good. He didn't deserve it.

Because he was right. I was here to see him, to show him what he had missed out on if he was really with Evelyn last night. If he had been, then he would never get to be inside me ever again.

"No back talk this time, Butterfly?" he taunted. "I must be right."

Butterfly?!

Heat coursed through my body.

"You're not ri—"

Before I could finish my sentence, he pushed another finger into me. I glared back at him, wanting to show him that he didn't affect me in the slightest, that his fingers didn't even feel *that* good inside me, that he wasn't as alpha as he thought he was.

"Keep fumbling on those words," he murmured. "It's almost as cute as when you're choking on my dick down your throat."

"Fuck you," I gritted out.

"You know what I love about brats like you?" he murmured. "How wet they get when they're being punished. How tight their pussy wraps around my fingers when I punish them for their disrespectful mouth."

"Was my mouth disrespectful, wrapped around your cock the other night?" I snarled.

"Butterfly, you were sucking on my cock like it was a fucking pacifier." He pushed a third finger into my pussy and massaged my G-spot. "Don't act like you didn't enjoy being filled. You should be honored to be filled with your master's dick."

"You'd never fucking be my master. Ever."

"Say it again." He chuckled lowly in my ear. "Your pussy gets tight when you lie."

I shoved my shoulder back, wanting to struggle against him and put up a fight because he didn't deserve to have this much power over me. But he moved his hand to the small of my back, easily keeping me in place.

"I hope that she was worth it last night," I said, face pressed against the wood.

"Who?"

"Evelyn."

"What the fuck are you talking about?" Hector growled into my ear, pumping his fingers into me faster. "You're the only woman I'm seeing."

While her being at Radiant didn't mean anything and I could definitely be blowing this out of proportion, Eric had stressed me out yesterday, and Evelyn was Instagram-model pretty, even without all the filters.

"She was at Radiant last night. Why else would she be there? She's working under—"

After wrapping his hand around the front of my throat, he lifted me off the desk and pressed his mouth against my ear. "Listen to me closely, Heather. If I had fucked her last night, I wouldn't be risking the entire relationship I'd built with your father to sneak around with you. I wouldn't be fucking you over my desk with the door unlocked, hoping he didn't walk in. And I certainly wouldn't have been waiting until midnight for you to meet me last night."

My eyes widened slightly, but I gritted my teeth together. "You're lying."

Had he really stayed until midnight last night just for me? And I had blown him off.

"If one more bratty thing comes out of your mouth, I'm tying you to the wall, fastening a vibrator against your clit, and watching you come over and over until you beg me to stop. Not at Radiant. Right here." He pointed to the wall near the door, across from his desk. "There."

"That doesn't sound like a punishment to—"

Hector pulled his fingers out of me, seized me by the elbow, and dragged me to the wall. Like a feral animal, he pulled the painting that I remembered him buying in Switzerland while on vacation with my family three years ago right off the goddamn wall and dropped it on the floor beside us.

Once he untied the tie from around my elbows, he fastened my wrists above my head to one of the nails that held up the painting. I struggled to escape, pulling on the tie in an attempt to loosen it, as he walked back to his desk.

"Let me out," I growled.

Opening his desk drawer, he pulled out a dildo, even bigger than him.

"Why do you have a dildo in your desk drawer?"

"Perks of having a sister who runs a sex shop," he mumbled under his breath.

After walking over to me, he rubbed the head of the dildo between my pussy lips and against my clit. I sucked in a sharp breath and looked toward the door, hoping that nobody would walk into the room.

"Hector," I said unsteadily, "let me out."

Instead of answering me, he pushed the dildo into my cunt. My pussy formed around it and gripped the thick toy, desperate to be filled after Hector ruthlessly pulled his fingers out of me. I pulled on the restraints, aching for his hands to be on me too.

He tightened the bind on my wrist. "I need to grab something."

My eyes widened. "What?! You're going to leave me here?!"

No response.

"Hector!" I whisper-yelled.

While I stood, nearly naked and tied to his wall, Hector walked toward the door.

"You can't leave me alone like this!" I exclaimed, yanking on the restraints.

At this angle, the dildo that he thrust into my pussy began slipping out of me. I pressed my thighs together in a weak attempt to keep it inside me and whimpered at how full I felt right now, completely helpless …

"Still not sticking to your word, huh?" I hummed, unable to stop the words from leaving my mouth. I had no control here, yet I was willing to say whatever to make him stay. "Where's the vibrator you said you'd fasten to me? Don't have one to—"

"Don't let that toy fall out of you." He stopped at the door. "Or I'll bring you out into the main office once your father leaves so everyone can see how much of a dirty slut you are for your father's best friend."

And with that, he walked out the door.

But that asshole would be back.

CHAPTER
THIRTEEN

HEATHER

WRISTS BOUND ABOVE MY HEAD, I stared up at them and tried to undo the binds before Hector returned. I was nearly naked in the middle of his unlocked office and didn't have an excuse if my father walked right in and saw me.

The door opened, and I sucked in a breath.

Hector walked back into the room. "Shit out of luck."

I pulled on the restraints. "Let me out."

"Vibrator isn't in my car like I thought it was, so you'll be punished in other ways."

With my pussy gripping the dildo tightly so it wouldn't fall out of me, I ground my teeth together and glared at Hector just waltzing into the room and finding a seat on the couch. He kicked his feet up on the coffee table.

"You can't do this to me," I cried.

"If you're any louder, your father will hear you."

"Hector!" I whisper-yelled across the room. "Let me out."

The toy slipped another inch out of me, and I desperately tried to push it back up into me with my thighs without much luck.

While I could've let it fall onto the ground, it eased some of the ache between my thighs.

Just a bit.

Hector glanced at my legs. "If you let that fall out of your pussy, you're going to regret it."

We glared at each other for a couple of moments—or more like I glared at him while he smirked at me and didn't make a move to leave the couch, to stand up, or to make another comment about my attitude.

Another inch of the dildo slipped out of my wet pussy, and I clenched around it.

He dropped his gaze to it, as if he was just waiting.

When the last inch of the dildo slipped out of my pussy and landed on the floor beneath me, I whimpered from the sudden feeling of emptiness, anticipating what he would do to me.

Yet he just looked at it, then up at me. And didn't move. Not an inch.

"So much for a punishment, huh?" I taunted.

How was he giving empty threats and thinking that I'd be a good girl for him? If he wanted to punish me, then he would have to do better than this. Especially after seeing Evelyn at Radiant last night, then again in his office with him, alone.

Instead of stalking over to me, he stared at me from across the room and smirked.

No response.

"I thought the big, bad Master was going to punish me," I said.

He chuckled.

I flared my nostrils. "Couldn't think of anything better than tying me up and watching me?"

Again, that asshole said nothing.

And then … then he had the freaking audacity to yawn!

The longer I stood with my arms tied over my head and my pussy suddenly empty, the more my cunt ached to be full again. I had held the dildo inside me for so, so long with my pussy gripping on to it tightly. Now nothing.

"Hector," I gritted out in an attempt to hide the ache.

Instead of answering me, he unbuckled his belt and reached into his pants. Heat exploded through my core, and I whimpered as he pulled out his huge, veiny, throbbing cock. Fuck, I wanted him inside me so badly.

"You see what you're missing now?" he asked. "A dick to fill that empty pussy."

After spitting on his hand, he glided his fingers over the head of his cock and made it glisten. I tried hard to grind my thighs together because I so desperately needed him to fuck me right here and right now. But he wasn't going to.

This was my punishment for not showing up at Radiant last night.

He wrapped his hand around the head of his dick, then slowly moved it downward until it met his balls. Then, he moved his hand back up, using his pre-cum almost like lube, letting it cover his cock.

"Fuck," I whispered.

With his eyes on me, he leaned back on the couch to relax and jerked himself off even faster. A low grunt escaped his throat. My jaw slackened, and I attempted to move my thighs together, craving him.

"Please," I pleaded.

"Please what?"

I opened and shut my mouth a handful of times, mesmerized by the way he stroked his dick and wanting it inside of me. My pussy was so empty, and he would fill it with his huge cock and with all that cum in his balls.

"I want your cum," I whimpered.

He stroked himself faster. "You want me to come?"

"Inside me."

"I'll come, but not inside you," he grunted, his dress shirt tightening around his huge biceps. And I couldn't handle the way it seemed to bulge. He groaned, "You haven't earned it yet."

He continued to jerk himself off, staring at my naked body, lips forming an O.

"Fuck," he grunted. "You're so fucking sexy, Heather."

A whimper left my mouth. "Hector …"

"Moan my name again, and I'll come for you."

"Come inside me," I said.

"Moan my name again," he growled.

"Hector," I breathed out.

Hector stiffened and came into his hand, grunting and cursing underneath his breath. All while my pussy was pulsing, the warmth gushing inside it and the wetness now coating my thighs. I needed him so badly that I began panting like a freaking dog for him.

"Please. Please. Please. Please. Please, Hector," I begged.

He stuffed himself back into his pants, walked over to me, and hovered his hand, filled with his cum, millimeters from my cunt. And while he was so close, he made no move to touch me. Not one.

"Please, Hector. Please, give it to me. I need it." I stared up at him. "Please. Please. Please. Please. Touch me. Use me. Collar me. I need you so badly right now. My body can't handle it." The words tumbled out of my mouth before I could stop them, but I meant each word.

I had only really read about Doms collaring their subs, but a couple of weeks ago, Hector had mentioned over messages that he wanted to collar me.

And, God, I wanted it.

Because it'd solve all my problems. Like Evelyn.

Hector stepped closer to me, his dick back in his pants and his free hand in his pocket.

"Please," I whispered, staring up at him through my lashes. "Collar me."

"If you want my collar around your neck, you have to earn it."

"Please, I'll do anything," I panted.

After curling his lips into a smirk, he shook his head. "You think you can disrespect me and then ask to be collared? Not show up at Radiant last night and then expect me to fuck you?" He moved closer so his mouth pressed against my ear. "No."

"Hector," I cried. "Please."

"No."

"Please, Sir."

Hector stiffened beside me and pushed his bulge against my thigh. "Are we learning?"

I bit back the bratty urge to say no and nodded.

"No." He lifted my chin with one finger. "I don't think so."

"I am," I said, nodding like a madwoman to convince him. "I'm learning to be a good submissive for you, Sir." Warmth gathered between my thighs at how close he finally was to me. "I'll do anything to make you happy. Anything to please my Master."

Instead of pushing his fingers into me, he stepped away. "Good. You can stay here—"

"No!" I cried, yanking on the restraints. "You're supposed to fuck me. Not walk away!"

"I'm not going to fuck you tonight," he said. "Maybe not tomorrow."

"Hector," I whimpered. "Please."

"I had plans to tie you up and force you to come over and over and over at Radiant last night, but you didn't want to show up. So, you're going to take this punishment tonight. And if you don't get yourself off all night, I'll think about allowing you to come tomorrow."

Biting my lip so I wouldn't tell him off, I glared at him and that stupid smirk.

"So, be a good girl."

CHAPTER
FOURTEEN

HECTOR

SITTING in my high-rise that overlooked Pittsburgh, I glanced across the table at Heather, who slammed her knife into the steak I'd made her after she finally calmed down back at the office and agreed to be good for me.

"Do you need help with that?" I asked.

"No," she growled sharply. "I'm perfectly capable."

After finally cutting off the first piece, she popped it into her mouth. Then, she wiped her face with a napkin and gazed at the bright city lights dancing in the night sky. "I can't believe you're making me go an entire day without coming."

While a statement like that from any other submissive would've annoyed me, I liked playing this little game with Heather. I highly doubted that she'd actually be able to not touch herself all night, and I couldn't wait to punish her for it tomorrow.

I swished some tequila in my mouth and swallowed it. "Why do you want to be collared?"

I had collared submissives before in the past and had been with them under a contract, but none of them had asked me to collar them as quickly as Heather had, especially after she had been giving me the cold shoulder since last night.

"So I can be the only one that you're with," Heather said, as if it were obvious.

My hand tightened around the glass. "That's a terrible reason."

Heather snapped her gaze up to mine, then narrowed her eyes. "Excuse me?"

"You heard me loud and clear, Heather."

After sending me daggers across the table, she crossed her arms. "It's not a good enough reason that I want to be the only woman that you're fucking? Noted. I'll go find someone else to sleep around with then too. You know there's this guy in my—"

I growled at the brattiness coming out of her mouth. She would be with nobody else and would definitely learn not to even have those fucking thoughts, period. Heather was all mine, and I refused to let anyone else have her.

"I'm not going to collar you," I clarified, "because you haven't earned it."

"What do you mean, I haven't earned it?!" she exclaimed, leaning forward. "I let you tie me up in your office while my father was in the other room and watched you come! If that doesn't mean I earned it, then I don't know what you want from me."

"I want you to listen to me."

"No, you don't," she said, leaning back. "You love putting me in my place."

I pressed my lips together because I couldn't argue with her. I loved having the power over her, but I wanted her to work for it, to show me—even though she was pissed at me for whatever reason last night—that she wouldn't abandon me.

As the thought crossed my mind, I stiffened. Out of all the women that I had been with before her, I never had to fear that they'd leave me. They might have not asked to be collared right away, but I had known they wouldn't leave.

But Heather?

She was much younger, bratty but intelligent, and my best friend's daughter.

She had a million reasons to leave me at any time. Hell, what would happen when she finally finished college? What about that guy she had asked her father to bring on vacation with us a couple of years ago? I knew nothing about her personal life or who she was involved with.

And it fucking terrified me to commit to an independent woman like her.

"Why are you so caught up on Evelyn?" I asked, realizing that her jealousy stemmed from her. "I already told you that—"

"Because she was at Radiant last night!" Heather snapped, then immediately turned away from me and crossed her arms over her chest, cheeks reddening. "That's why I'm so caught up on her, Hector."

"She was at Radiant last night?" I asked because I didn't remember seeing her.

"Don't play dumb with me," she said through her teeth, though her eyes were glistening under the candlelight. "She's the prettiest girl who works in your office, and she was at Radiant last night. I can put two and two together."

"You think I'm sleeping with her?"

"Yes, I think you're sleeping with her."

"I already told you that you're the only woman I'm with right now."

"Bullshit," she said. "You're handsome and successful, and I can't even pass a class."

So, that was still weighing on her mind.

I had given her no reason to be jealous of Evelyn—at least I didn't think I had—and while I might be successful, all my previous relationships hadn't worked out because I was so deep into my work that I didn't have much time to devote to my submissive than I would have liked. But that was already different with Heather.

She had made *me* wait for weeks before meeting because she wanted to study. She didn't message or call me at every hour of the day, wanting attention, though I would happily give it to her if she did. And she was playing hard to get.

Finally, she glanced over at me with tears trembling in her eyes. "Why was she there?"

I laid out my palm on the table, wanting her to take it. After peering down at it for a moment, she crossed her arms tighter around her body and pressed her lips together, as if she wasn't going to let me touch her.

And no touching for a guy whose love language was physical touch fucking stung.

After sighing, I pulled my hand away and sat up straight to shake off the sting of her rejection. Something about Heather drove me fucking mad, and I needed her acceptance, her touch, *her.*

"I don't know," I said.

"Of course you don't," she whispered, turning further away.

Gently cupping her chin, I turned her head toward me. "I'm telling you the truth."

"How can I trust you?" She pressed her quivering lips together. "My mom trusted my dad, and look at what happened between them."

Fucking Jacob. He'd always been a player.

"Your dad's a dick sometimes." I shook my head. "I'll be the first to admit that."

As far as I knew, he put a lot more pressure on Heather than his son, but they still had a decent relationship after he broke up their family. Though the more I thought about why Evelyn had been at Radiant last night …

"I think your father and Evelyn are hooking up."

Heather probably didn't believe me in the slightest because it sounded like I was trying to make an excuse for myself and for her, but it was the truth. Evelyn had looked so uncomfortable in front of me while that hum was buzzing through the room.

And if Michelle had taught me anything about sex toys from her business, it was that the hum of her most popular vibrator sounded exactly fucking like that.

"What?" Heather asked.

I furrowed my brows, then shook my head to push the thought away. If Jacob was really sleeping with one of our interns and HR found out about it, I didn't know what was going to happen to the company or to his stake in it.

"Forget it for now," I said. I'd deal with that tomorrow. "Did you talk to your professor?"

"Yes," she said, eyes narrowed, still pissed at me about not letting her come.

"What'd he say?"

She pursed her lips together. "Don't worry about it."

"That's what he told you?"

"No. That's what I'm telling you because he told me that I can't do anything about it."

Somehow, I didn't think she was telling me the truth. She hadn't looked me in my eyes since I'd asked about her professor and now sat across from me, twiddling her thumbs way too aggressively to be telling the truth.

She jumped up from the table. "I'm going to use the bathroom."

"Heather," I warned, "if you touch yourself—"

She snickered. "Don't worry; I won't."

CHAPTER
FIFTEEN

HEATHER

DURING DINNER, I used the bathroom in Hector's high-rise because I really had to pee, and on my way back to the dining room, I might've peered into Hector's office because I was bored and desperate *not* to talk to him about what Eric had said to me yesterday. There was no way that I'd ever stoop that low to get him a job.

Once I made sure that he didn't notice me slip into the room, I gently shut the door behind me, not enough for it to click closed, but enough so he couldn't just walk in and see me all over his work.

I walked around the office and stared up at the large bookcase fixed on the opposite wall. Books and books and more books and no pictures of family. No sentimental items that he had kept from when he was a child. And definitely no evidence that he had any interest in Evelyn.

Just modern and minimalistic.

After running a hand over my head, I blew out a breath. What was wrong with me? Sane Heather would've never accused someone of cheating on her even though we weren't even a couple yet. But with Hector ... my possessiveness came out.

Pursing my lips together, I walked over to his desk. Nothing here either. Except ...

A sticky note with my name, stuck on a stack of papers.

I grazed my fingers across the pages and swallowed hard, wondering if I should open it. After all, it *did* have my name written across the sticky note. That meant that it was for me, and now, my curiosity was piqued.

So, after glancing over my shoulder, I flipped open the document.

Dominant and Submissive Agreement

This contract is entered into by Hector Patton (hereinafter referred to as Master) and Heather Hodge (hereinafter referred to as submissive) on the ______ of November. Master and submissive agree to enter into an exclusive BDSM relationship.

Holy shit, did he have a contract for us already drafted? What happened to him not wanting to collar me because he didn't think I deserved it? And all this goddamn time, there was already a contract drafted on his desk?!

Safeword

Master and submissive will use ________ (hereinafter referred to as safeword). If the safeword is spoken at any time before, during, or after a sexual act, then Master and submissive will stop performing right away and begin aftercare. For any act where Master or submissive cannot speak verbally, they will consecutively squeeze the other's thumb four times.

Responsibilities

The responsibilities of Master include:

1. *To respect submissive's soft and hard limits.*
2. *To help submissive improve sexually.*
3. *To reward good behavior.*
4. *To perform aftercare.*
5. *To ensure that each scene is safe for submissive.*
6. *To provide housing, meals, and any essential item that submissive might need.*

The responsibilities of submissive include:

1. *To refer to Master as Master or Sir.*
2. *To ask permission to come.*
3. *To follow Master's directions.*
4. *To be loyal to Master.*

Neither party shall be allowed to form a sexual relationship with anyone else until the agreement is terminated by either the Master or the submissive. Submissive also agrees that she will surrender full control to Master during the term and will become a full-time submissive and there will be a total power exchange between Master and submissive.

I arched a brow. Full-time submissive? Total power exchange? Who did he think I was? If he had learned anything about me in the past few weeks that we'd been chatting online and for the past few years that we'd known each other, he'd know that I would *never* allow that.

No way was I letting a man run my life.

If submissive does not obey these rules, Master will enforce a punishment. Punishments will be as mild or as intense as the Master believes is required. Punishments can include, but are not limited to:

1. *Bondage in the form of rope, handcuffs, zip ties, clothing, or any other material.*
2. *Physical punishment, including spanking, caning, paddling, or with the use of other tools.*

3. *Orgasm control. Master shall control submissive's orgasms, giving or refusing them.*
4. *Public discipline. Submissive might be required to masturbate in public, wear revealing clothing, or let her Master walk her on a leash.*
5. *Degradation. Master shall use submissive as a worthless slave if he deems it appropriate and shall require submissive to walk around with her Master's cum dripping down her thighs, referring to herself as a dirty whore while at Radiant, letting other Dominants write insults on her body, and more.*
6. *Saddles.*

Heat exploded through my core, and I pressed my thighs together. I didn't know what he thought was actually a punishment, but it definitely wasn't *any* of this. If he did any of these things to me, I'd probably come on the spot.

But what did saddles mean? Weren't those the things someone put on a horse to ride it? And why wasn't there more of an explanation about that one, like all the others? Part of me felt like it should've been looped in with the physical punishments, but oh well.

I sat on one of the comfy chairs across from his desk, continuing down the page.

If Master deems that it's required, multiple forms of punishment might happen at once.

Oh? My lips curled into a smirk. What did I have to do to get multiple punishments?

The possibilities raced through my head, and I found myself crossing my legs in an attempt to stop the ache growing in my core. I had promised Hector I wouldn't touch myself, and I planned to keep that promise so he'd let me come tomorrow.

But what would multiple punishments at once even look like?

Underneath the Punishment section, I read the words *soft limits* and *hard limits* with a block of empty space. I chewed on the inside of my cheek and continued reading, nervous because I didn't even know what I'd put under my limits.

I knew nothing about sex.

Okay, well, I knew *some* things, but not as much as Hector.

Privacy

This agreement is confidential and may not be shared with anyone, except legal counsel.

Termination

This agreement is legally binding and will last indefinitely or until either party terminates the agreement. Any party can terminate this agreement at any time. However, if either party terminates this agreement, this agreement and the relationship dynamic will remain confidential and private indefinitely.

Indefinitely? I chewed on the inside of my cheek. Hector was thinking long-term and monogamously, and here I was, accusing him of cheating because I was insecure and stressed about that damn software coding class.

Suddenly, someone cleared their throat behind me, and I whipped my head around to see Hector leaning against the doorframe with his hands stuffed into his pockets and his dark eyes fixed on me.

"What are you doing in here, Heather?"

HEATHER

AFTER TWIRLING all the way around and hiding the contract behind my back, I stepped backward and bumped into his desk. "Nothing!" I exclaimed, then slid onto it, regaining some of my composure from him surprising me.

He stepped into the room and gently shut the door behind him. "Nothing, huh?"

"Nope," I said, popping the *P*.

"And what is behind your back?"

"You know," I hummed, "just a contract with my name on it."

Stiffening, Hector dropped his gaze to his desk and then lifted it back up to mine. Heat grew warmer between my thighs, as all I could think about was that Hector was so serious about this— *about us*—that he had already drafted a contract.

A freaking BDSM contract!

"Is that so?" Hector asked, stalking closer to me with that dangerous look in his eye, like the one he had given me this afternoon at the office when he tied my hands over my head.

"Yep."

"Well, with that little smirk on your face, it seems like you're enjoying it." He moved around his desk, sat in the chair, and twirled me around so I faced him. "Why don't you read all your favorite parts to me?"

My eyes widened, and I shook my head. "I-I don't think—"

"Nonsense," he said, holding the contract in his hands now. "Read it."

"Okay, fine," I said, reading it through my head.

He growled. "Aloud."

Fuck.

I stared down at the contract and flipped to the Responsibilities section, leaning back on one hand. He shifted my legs so mine were spread and his were nestled between them, his bulge on full freaking display underneath the dim light flooding in through the large windows.

"My favorite part is responsibility number three," I said. "Where you reward me."

"You only get rewarded for good behavior."

"I'm always good."

"I'd say the opposite."

"Well, that's *your* opinion," I said. "I am good ... just not for you."

"Rewards only come if *I* think you've been good. Not the other way around." After standing, he flipped to *the responsibilities of submissive* section and took my chin in his hand. "You will refer to me as Master or Sir. You always ask for permission to come. You follow my directions. And you stay loyal to me, Heather. Is that understood?"

I stared up at him, excitement rushing through me. "Or what?"

He moved closer to me, his bulge millimeters from my pussy. "Or you'll be punished."

"I've read the Punishment section already," I said.

"So you know what will happen when you talk back to me."

I bit back a smirk. "They're all my favorite."

"None of them should be your favorite," he growled. "They're punishments."

"Oh yeah." I giggled. "I mean that I hate them all. Especially the public discipline one."

It seemed hot on paper, but if he actually made me do that in real life, I would probably have another freaking heart attack, like I did today at the office! Though I would never ever tell him that or he'd use it to his full advantage.

"You won't enjoy the punishment when I force you through twenty consecutive orgasms and refuse to stop until you're calling yourself a dirty little whore on the saddle," he said.

He pressed his dick against my aching pussy, and I whimpered.

Screw these being my favorite! This orgasm control was killing me already. Once I'd had a taste of how Hector could make me feel, I so desperately wanted more … and more … and more. And to be a good girl to get it? Un-fucking-real!

"Hector," I whispered, pussy pulsing. "Please."

"Please what?"

"Let me touch myself. Let me come."

"Are we making demands now?" he asked. "That's no way to ask to feel good."

"N-no!" I said, shaking my head, spreading my legs further, and deciding to start over. I didn't think I could handle another freaking hour of this constant teasing from him, knowing I could do nothing. "I mean, can I come, please?"

"Please what?"

"Please, Sir."

He pressed his bulge harder against me. "No."

"Please," I cried, staring down at the way his dick ground against my underwear over and over and over, stains now covering his pants from my wetness. "Please, I'm begging you, Sir. I need it so badly. I can't wait until tomorrow."

"No."

I placed my feet up on the desk, wanting to grind back against him.

Before I could move an inch, he stopped. "You know what'll happen if you make yourself feel good, don't you? You won't get to come tomorrow. Or the next day. Or the next. Your punishment will continue until you learn to be good."

"But I am good," I whispered, not grinding against him, but close to it. "Please, let me."

"No."

My bottom lip quivered, and I stared up at him through big eyes. "Please."

"My answer is not going to change, Heather," he said. "Only I can make you feel good tonight. If I want to make you come, that'll be my choice based on how good you are for me. And you're not proving to be a good girl tonight."

"I'm good," I whimpered. "I'm good. I'm good. I haven't touched myself at all."

"You're going to wait for it," he said.

"B-but, Sir …"

He snatched my chin in his hand, pressed his bulge back against my pussy, and ground himself into me. "You are going to wait for it, or I'll add another day to your punishment. Do I make myself clear?"

A wave of heat coursed through my body, and I swallowed hard.

Another day?! I can't even last a couple of hours!

"Yes," I whispered.

And when I didn't address him properly, he lifted my chin. "Yes?"

"Yes, Sir." I glanced down at his huge bulge, wishing that he'd rip off his pants and thrust himself inside of me because, damn, I needed it badly. "I'll wait until you think I've earned it. I'll be a good girl for you until tomorrow."

And then, once I got what I wanted, I'd act however I damn well pleased.

HEATHER

"BLACK COFFEE," Mom said, standing beside me at Carnegie Coffee Company.

I glanced over at Sierra, Athena, and Sun, who sat in our usual seat in the corner of the café. We had been people-watching all afternoon while I impatiently waited for Hector to text me when to meet him at Radiant.

While I believed that he wasn't sleeping with Evelyn, I didn't want to walk in and see her there again. My insecurities would run rampant, and I might even run right out of the club and go back home to masturbate my troubles away.

Especially since Hector hadn't touched me last night, and now, I was cranky.

"What do you want, honey?" she asked.

"I'm good. I already have a cookie back at my seat." I nervously looked back over at my friends again, wishing that I could just grow up and give Mom the contract to look over. I was twenty-four and still felt so awkward around my parents while talking about sex. "So ... thanks for coming."

"Of course," she said, waving at the others. "What's going on?"

With my lips pursed, I stared at her for a long, long time.

"Black coffee!" the barista yelled.

"Hmm?" Mom asked, grabbing it and taking a sip.

"If I had a contract that I needed reviewed, would you be okay looking through it?"

"What's it for?"

"Um ..." I rocked back on my heels. "You know what? Never mind."

"Is it a work contract?"

"More like a personal one."

"A personal one?"

"Okay, okay. You know how you told me that I could tell you anything?" I asked, chewing on the inside of my cheek. "Well, if I show you, then you have to promise not to say anything to anyone, especially Dad."

"Lawyer-client confidentiality."

"I might or might not have a ... BDSM contract that I've been offered," I squeaked.

While I expected Mom to shriek, she stared at me, wide-eyed, for a few moments, then suddenly, she curled one arm around my shoulders and pulled me toward her. "Taking after her mama. I've been waiting for this day. Did you finally lose your virgini—"

My cheeks burned red. "Mom!"

She giggled. "What?"

I scrunched my nose at her. "Ew, was that how you and Dad ..."

"Met? At a sex club?" She smirked. "And ten months later, you popped out."

"Ew."

"So, who's the guy?"

"Nobody."

"One of your friends?"

"No."

"Someone at college?"

"No."

"Is it a girl?"

"No!" My entire body felt like it was in flames. "Can you drop it, please?"

After rolling her eyes, she took another sip. "Give it to me, and I'll take a look at it."

"Promise you won't tell Dad?"

"Heather, I don't even see him anymore," she said.

"You have to promise."

"Fine. I promise."

"Good."

After grabbing the contract Hector had given me last night from my bag, I jogged back over to Mom and handed it to her. He told me to have someone look it over to explain anything that I had more questions on, to make sure I was comfortable.

And I had made sure to white-out his name before bringing it here today.

No freaking way would I give it to Mom with his name written across it.

"I'll look it over tonight," she said, phone buzzing. "I have to take this. Love you."

Once she left, I walked back to my seat and slumped down against the chair.

Maybe I shouldn't have handed it over to her. What if she chips off the white-out and sees Hector Patton *written in multiple places?! She knows who he is, was with Dad when they started out as business partners.*

"Did you give her the contract?" Athena asked.

"Maybe …"

"What'd she say?" Sun asked. "How'd you tell her it is with Hector?"

"By not telling her."

"But isn't his name all over it?"

"I whited it out."

Athena looked at Sun, and Sun furrowed her brows.

"No, you didn't."

"Yes, I did," I said. "Last night."

Athena leaned closer. "When you showed it to us five minutes ago, it had his name."

Blood drained from my face. "Shut up. You're lying. It did—"

"Is that your dad?" Sierra asked, leaning close to me and out the window.

Suddenly stressed the fuck out, I followed her gaze. Sure enough, across the street, my father stepped out of his car and opened the passenger seat door for … *Evelyn*. My eyes widened as his arm curled around her waist, and he whispered something in her ear, causing her to go red.

"Welp …"

"Is he with someone?" Sun said, squinting her eyes.

"Do you need glasses?" Athena said.

"No," Sierra said. "They're just too far away."

"If you can't see them clearly, then you definitely need glasses, Sun. Their faces are clear to me."

"Shush it!" I exclaimed. "They're coming this way …"

HEATHER

WHAT THE HELL?! *Why is Dad here?*

I shrank down in my seat and held my coffee cup over my face, as if that would shield them from seeing me. In the middle of the goddamn street, Dad kissed Evelyn on the jaw, his fingers moving up her waist and to her breast, and I averted my gaze immediately.

If they were seeing each other, that meant two things. One, I had made a complete ass out of myself around Hector, blaming him. Two, I had to be more careful at Radiant if my father apparently went there, too, with Evelyn since I had seen her there just the other night.

While I didn't want him to notice me, I creepily watched them walk into Carnegie Coffee Company, Dad's hand set on Evelyn's waist and her cheeks rounded slightly, nipples taut through her shirt.

Oh my God. My eyes are burning.

First, Mom. Now, this?

After making eye contact with me while Dad ordered, Evelyn stiffened and turned back to him. I turned my head away and hoped that he wouldn't look over here, too, because that would be awkward for the both of us.

"Oh my God," I mumbled under my breath.

"Who is that with him?" Sierra asked.

I sank down further in my seat. "His assistant."

"His assistant?" Sierra asked, then wiggled her brows. "Or his *assistant?*"

Slapping a hand over my forehead, I tore my gaze away from them and stared at my phone, specifically at my messages with Hector. If I looked at my email from that stupid professor, who was way too young to be a professor, I'd be pissed. If I looked any further up at Dad, I'd be grossed the hell out.

So, I settled for torturing myself at the thought of Hector tonight.

As if he had known I was thinking about him, a message popped up on the screen. More specifically, an image. Of one of the glass rooms at Radiant. A bed. Thick black rope. And something that looked like a saddle to ride a horse.

"Heather," Dad said.

I slammed my screen down on the table, earning a stifled giggle from Sierra, and looked up to see Dad now standing a couple of feet away from Evelyn and staring at me. Evelyn tucked some hair behind her ear and shuffled nervously beside him.

"Oh, hey, Dad." *The hell?!* "What're you doing here?"

"Grabbing some coffee after work," Dad said, walking over to the table.

"Oh, really?" I hummed.

Because we were pretty damn far from downtown Pittsburgh, where he had his office, and that hugging and kissing had looked a little bit more than just friendly business partners grabbing some coffee after work.

"Sorry I couldn't make it today," I said.

"Don't worry about it, sweetheart. Hector was asking for you though."

My eyes widened, and I perked up. "He was?"

"I heard that you didn't do too well on your last test in your software development class," Dad said, and I suppressed the urge to roll my eyes that Hector had told Dad *that*, but at least it wasn't the other thing. "He's helping you out?"

"Yes."

Sierra smirked at me from across the table, her back facing Dad so he couldn't see her face, and then mouthed, *In more than one way.*

I kicked her and tried hard for my cheeks not to redden. "Yeah."

"You could've asked your brother for help."

For some reason, Evelyn stiffened when Dad mentioned Aaron, and I wondered just how freaky that girl really was. Dad noticed and stood back up, a small smirk written across his face, and I kept the blankest expression that I could …

Because what the fuck was that?!

"Yeah, well …" I trailed off, slinking down in the seat. "He's busy being successful."

"That's how your brother is," Dad said, squeezing my shoulder. "He'll make time for you."

After dropping my gaze to the table, I blew out a breath, my bangs blowing up into the air. "All right, well"—*as much as I love this conversation that is about to take a turn into how great Aaron is*—"I have to get studying."

"See you later, sweetheart," Dad called, stepping back.

Once they walked out of Carnegie Coffee Company, they walked down the stairs and kept their distance from each other all the way until they reached Dad's car. I turned back to the group, who giggled away over their steeped tea, slices of carrot cake, and latte art.

"All this time," I whispered, "I thought Evelyn was fucking Hector."

"Turns out, she's just fucking your dad." Sierra snickered.

Athena smirked. "And your brother."

"Did you see the way she stiffened when your dad mentioned him?" Sierra asked.

"Listen." Sun, the quietest one out of all of us, giggled. "Props to her if she's getting fucked by both of them."

"Ew," I said, scrunching my nose even harder. "I don't even want that thought in my head, never mind the image of it."

"She seems like she keeps to herself," Sun commented.

"We should ask her if she wants to be friends," Athena said.

"I don't think she'd fit in," Sun said.

"Yeah, true, we're all virgins, except Heather," Athena said.

"And Sierra," I added.

"Heather!" Sierra exclaimed. "That's supposed to be a secret."

"Ooh," Athena said. "You have some tea to spill, Sierra?"

"No!" Sierra glared in my direction. "At least not in public."

My phone buzzed on the table, and I turned it over to see another message from Hector.

Hector: Make sure you eat before you come to Radiant. You're going to need the energy for tonight. Especially if I find out that you need to be punished because I won't go easy on you.

Hector: Tonight, you'll see what it means to be my submissive.

CHAPTER
NINETEEN

HECTOR

AFTER DRESSING the bed in a new set of sheets, I smoothed out the comforter and then leaned back, imagining Heather sprawled out on this bed tonight, her body glistening in sweat and cum.

I walked over to the dresser and pulled open the drawer of my favorite rope.

Plaything Co. Bondage Rope.

Like all the other toys she had given me, Michelle had *donated* nearly twenty samples of rope to me when she was choosing which one to add to her online sex shop. I pulled the smooth black rope out and let one strand fall to the ground. This one was sturdy, reliable, and easy on the skin.

My phone lit up on the stand, and I glanced down at the messages.

Heather: Hmm ...

A smile twitched on my lips. I had been impatiently waiting for tonight since yesterday, when I had given her strict orders not to touch herself. And while I was the Dom and I gave the orders, I had given myself the same punishment.

No coming. No jerking off.

Not until she learned.

It was a way to reward us both—her for listening and me for teaching her well.

Heather: What are the punishments again?

Hector: Don't test me, Heather.

Because I liked it too much. Especially from her.

Heather: I promise I don't need any punishment.

After drawing my tongue across my teeth, I shook my head and placed the phone down on the dresser. I laid the rope on the bed and grabbed the saddle from the closet, setting it in the center of the mattress.

Oh, Heather, Heather, Heather …

She knew exactly what she was doing to me, and I fucking loved it.

I found myself thinking about her more than I should've throughout the day, and I feared that, one day, this would all be over because it couldn't last forever with her father being my business partner and best friend.

And when this was over, I'd be ruined for anyone else.

I wouldn't find anyone like Heather ever again.

Once I grabbed a bottle of water and some snacks from the other room, I set them on a side table, dimmed the lights, and headed out to the front to wait for her. Only a few more minutes, and I'd finally get to tie her down and pleasure her the way I'd always wanted.

Since Heather wasn't here yet—*she'd better show up*—I spotted Michelle and Steven sitting on a maroon couch by the bar. I stuffed one hand in my pocket and walked toward them while scanning the bar for Heather.

When I reached them, Michelle looked up at me. "Where have you—"

"No more fucking dildos in my office," I growled at her.

Michelle snickered. "Did Heather find it and think you like being pegged?"

I gritted my teeth and glared at her. "Don't bring them anymore."

"Well, who is going to test my products?" she asked.

"If you have rope you want me to test, fine. Saddles, fine. But if you bring in a fucking dildo to my office ever again, I'm going to throw it out the window, and you'll be responsible if it hits anyone on the way down."

"Wooooow," Michelle said. "Don't even want to support your sister's small biz."

I looked over at Steven. "How do you deal with this?"

Steven chuckled. "Patience."

After gritting my teeth, I turned my glare on my sister. "Well, I have none for you."

"Makes sense," Michelle said, tilting her head the way she did right before she was about to try therapy on me that she'd learned in college twenty fucking years ago. "You crave control, but now, you have a sub who hates giving it to you. Your patience is thinning with me, so you can provide—"

"I need a fucking drink." I grabbed one from the passing waiter and sat beside Steven. "From here on out, I'm going to tune her out whenever she gets into the therapy talk because I can't deal with her diagnosing me."

Because she was spot-on every single fucking time.

And I hated it.

"Ah, the therapy talk." Steven chuckled. "I got that last month."

"Well, if either of you actually went to a therapist, I wouldn't have to put my expertise to the test." She sat on the edge of the couch and crossed her legs. "You know, talking to someone could be really healthy for both of you, could help clear your minds."

"I clear my mind by—"

"Fucking your sub?" Michelle smirked. "Isn't that her, standing by the bar and talking to—"

Before she could even finish her sentence, I twisted my head to see Heather standing at the bar with a teal-colored drink in her hand and Jameson Hart next to her … *flirting*. I gritted my teeth and stormed over to her.

"Heather," I growled to myself. "If this is her way of teasing me …"

"Do you know where Hector is?" she asked Jameson.

Jameson's gaze lifted to mine, and he cleared his throat and nodded past her.

I curled my arm around Heather's waist and drew her toward me. "Jameson."

"Hector, we were just—"

"She's mine," I said, cutting him off because Jameson loved to flirt with anyone.

But I wasn't letting *anyone* else have Heather.

"I was just asking him where you were …" Heather trailed off.

Not wanting any ogling eyes on us, I twirled Heather around and headed for the glass rooms so nobody would see us together —or see how possessive I was over her. For fuck's sake, her father now came here after I idiotically mentioned it to him a few months back. And now, I had to ensure that he didn't see me with his daughter.

Heather widened her eyes and pushed her thighs together. "What was that?"

"That was me not liking the way he was looking at you."

She smirked. "You're acting jealous."

After opening the door to my room for the night, I followed her inside and shut the door. "You're right. I'm jealous because I don't want any other man to even think about you the way that I do." I stalked closer to her. "You're all mine."

TWENTY

HEATHER

"IF YOU'RE that possessive over me"—I smirked—"maybe you should collar me."

Hector drew his tongue across his teeth, his hand slithering from my elbow, up my arm, and then around the front of my neck, as if it were a collar. "I already told you that you'll be collared when you've earned it."

I batted my lashes and shuffled backward until my legs hit the bed. "But I have been."

"No, you followed one of my orders," he clarified. "Haven't you?"

"Maybe …" I said, rocking back on my heels and into the bed.

"You haven't touched yourself all day?" Hector asked.

"Nope."

He raised an eyebrow. "Are you lying to me?"

"Nope." When he didn't say anything further, I smiled up at him. "I'm being serious."

"How come I don't believe you?" he asked.

"Because you have trust issues."

A low chuckle escaped his throat, and he popped off the first button of my shirt. "Correct." Another button. "I do have trust issues, especially when known brats promise me that they're speaking the truth."

Warmth grew between my legs. "I am."

Once he popped off all my buttons, he tugged my shirt off my shoulders and let it fall to our feet. Then, he unclipped my bra. The straps fell down my shoulders, my breasts sliding out of the cups. Hector's gaze dropped to them for a moment, and I could feel his dick hardening against me.

"Mmhmm …"

Next, he slid off my pants, his hands moving all the way down my legs. I stepped out of the clothes, and he set them on a cushioned chair in the corner of the room while I stood naked in front of him, slowly falling into—what Hector had mentioned on one of our many messages before we met—subspace.

After Hector pulled my arms behind my back, he slithered some rope that had been lying on the bed around them, starting at my wrists and so agonizingly slowly working his way up my arms to past my elbows. I glanced over my shoulder and rubbed my thighs together.

"Sir," I whined. "Please, I've been waiting so long for it."

"Patience," he said, "makes the pleasure feel that much better."

"I don't have any more patience," I cried, throwing my head back. "Please."

He finished up with the knots and grabbed a second set of rope from the bed. "Sit."

With my arms tied behind my back, I slid my ass up onto the bed and scooched back until my legs were straight in front of me. Hector crawled up beside me and bent my leg until the back of my thigh touched my calf, and then he knotted the rope around my ankle.

Heat coursed through my body as the rope casually glided against my clit.

"Look at that pretty, drooling pussy," he murmured, working the rope up my thigh.

Once he finished with my right thigh, he dipped his hand between my legs and rubbed my cunt. I moaned, a wave of pleasure rushing through me at the first touch in *hours*, and lifted my hips so he'd touch more of me.

"You're aching for it, aren't you?" he asked.

"Yes," I cried. "Please, Sir."

"Bend your left leg."

I leaned back on my hands and bent my left leg.

Like he had done with my right leg, he knotted the rope around my ankle and then worked his way up my thigh, purposefully dragging the rope over my clit whenever he could. I lifted my hips every time, desperate to get any friction he'd give.

My pussy was drooling, my nipples were taut, and my entire body was aching.

"I'm completely at your mercy," I said when he finished. "Now, please …"

With ease, Hector picked me up off the bed and set me on top of what looked to be a saddle with a huge dildo attached to it on the bed. I hovered over it the best that I could, but since my legs were tied together, I couldn't stand in the tall kneeling position.

So, my body fell effortlessly back on the saddle and on the dildo, letting it fill me.

A moan escaped my mouth, and I settled onto it, so full.

Hector slipped off the bed and walked around it, pulling on his tie.

"Every time you come tonight, you thank me." Hector captured my chin. "Understand?"

I bit back the urge to say no and nodded.

Hector had full control right now, and if I said something bratty to him, he wouldn't let me come. And I had been waiting for what seemed like days now. Freaking days! All for him. I refused to wait any longer.

My gaze dropped to the bed.

"I need a verbal response, Heather."

"Yes, Sir."

"No," he growled, tightening his grasp on my chin. "You look at me when you answer."

"But isn't—"

"Isn't it more submissive to bow your head and show respect?" He finished my sentence. "Maybe with other Doms. But you answer to me, so your eyes are on mine. Whenever you ask questions. Whenever you respond to me. Whenever you come."

Warmth spread through my pussy. "Yes, Sir."

"Now …" He flicked on a button on the saddle, and suddenly, it came to life, vibrating underneath me and against my clit. I jerked up slightly, but the restraints held me still. "What are you going to do for me?"

"Thank you whenever I come tonight," I whispered, voice shaking.

He stroked my hair. "That's my good girl."

Panting, I sat on the saddle, my pussy drooling all over it.

"You've earned a reward," he said, turning the vibrations on higher.

My thighs gripped the saddle underneath me, the feeling of being full in front of Hector making my pussy tighten. I stared up at him, waiting for him to touch me, to grope my breasts, squeeze my nipples …

Anything.

Except he stepped away from the bed.

"Look how pretty and helpless you are."

The toy vibrated against my clit, driving me higher and higher.

He dropped his tie on the floor. "All for me."

"S-S-Sir," I cried, tugging on the restraints in an attempt to displace all the pleasure.

"You've been such a good girl." Then, he unbuttoned his dress shirt. "Such a good girl for me, Heather. All last night, you didn't touch yourself once, all because I'd told you not to." He turned the vibrations up. "You're so good at following my directions."

The pressure soared inside me.

He leaned over the bed, one hand posted on the mattress. His muscles rippled under the dim light. He hovered his mouth up the center of my chest between my breast, up the column of my neck, and then millimeters from my lips.

I teetered on the brink of an orgasm, brows furrowed, mouth open, and panting heavily. "S-S-Sir …"

When he pressed his lips against mine, I cried out into his mouth and came hard on the saddle, the pleasure shooting through my body in waves.

"Thank you, Sir. Thank you, Sir. Thank you, Sir," I said into our kiss.

He slipped his tongue into my mouth, swallowing my words.

"Thank you!" I cried, wave after wave still crashing through me.

"Good girl," he murmured against my lips. "That's one." He stepped away from me again and undid his belt buckle, sliding it off his hips and dropping it onto the ground. "How many more do you think you've earned tonight?"

My eyes rolled back. "A-a-all of them."

He chuckled and unzipped his pants. I lifted my hazy gaze to watch him slide off his pants and briefs, his huge cock springing out of them. I tightened around the dildo, the pressure building up inside me again.

Instead of wrapping his hand around himself like he had done yesterday, he walked over to the bed again. I stared down at his hard dick, nipples aching and pussy pulsing at the thought of him slamming it into me over and over again.

"Imagine how good I'll feel inside of your tight pussy," he said, crawling onto the bed.

I tightened.

"Pounding into you …"

I bit my lip hard and tried desperately to pull my gaze away from his dick, but I couldn't.

"Filling you to the brim with my cum all night ..."

"Please," I begged. "Please, give it to me! I've been a good girl!"

"Patience."

When he wrapped his hand around his cock and stroked it from base to tip, I lost it and came hard on the dildo for a second time.

"T-thank y-you, S-S-Sir!" I cried, body trembling uncontrollably. "Thank you for letting me come, Sir."

In the midst of my orgasm, he laced a hand through my hair and gently guided my head forward, bending me at the hip. Eagerly, I wrapped my mouth around the head of his cock and sucked on him hungrily, bobbing my head back and forth as best as I could from this position.

He wrapped his hand around the front of my throat and pushed himself into me as deep as he could, until my lips met his groin. Instead of pulling back, I stared up at him through hazy eyes, the pressure building up inside me.

"Fuck, you're so pretty with your lips wrapped around my cock like that."

I sucked harder on him, loving the feeling of being full in two holes.

"A hungry slut ..."

I squeezed my eyes shut, about to come for a third time.

He clicked his tongue.

"What would your father think if he knew how much of a hungry slut you were for me?"

I moaned out around his dick, eyes rolling back into my head. "Thank you for letting me come, Sir. Thank you for letting me come. Thank you for letting me come," I said, the tears building in my eyes from the pure intensity of the third orgasm in a row. "Thank you."

He lifted my head and set me back into a half kneel.

"You're doing so good," Hector praised, taking my nipples between his fingers.

When he tugged on them, I threw my head back and came again. Almost instantly.

"Oh my God!" I cried. "T-t-thank you, S-S-Sir."

"Do you see what you get when you're good for me?" he asked.

"Yes," I whispered.

A ferocious, hungry growl escaped Hector's mouth, and suddenly, he lifted me off the saddle and pushed it to the edge of the bed like a madman, the dildo covered in my juices and the hum of the vibrator still drifting through the room.

He shoved me onto my stomach. With my cheek pressed against the mattress, I looked over my shoulder and back at him as he undid the knots around my legs. Then, he crawled up and straddled my thighs, in a prone-bone position.

Once he slipped his dick between my thighs and positioned it at my entrance, he seized hold of the rope knotted around my arms and pulled up on it slightly so my shoulders lifted off the mattress. And then he slammed deep into me.

I threw my head back and moaned. "Oh my God!"

He held onto the knots and used them to pound deeper and faster into me.

My body jerked back and forth, my pussy empty and then full. Empty, then full. I clenched around him, building up to a fourth— fifth?—orgasm of the night. I had already lost count. My mind was so numb when my pussy was stuffed full.

"Are you going to be a good girl for me from now on?"

I bit my cheek, furrowed my brows, and stared back into those dark eyes.

He pulled the rope tighter. "Heather …"

"W-what?"

"I asked a question. I expect an answer."

"No," I said, filled with overwhelming delight as waves of pleasure rushed through me. "I'm going to be a bad girl."

Because, well, I had more fun that way.

TWENTY-ONE

HEATHER

AFTER HECTOR UNDID MY RESTRAINTS, he pulled me into his arms and walked with me to the bed. He laid me on his chest and gently drew his fingers through my hair, the rhythmic movement so soothing.

"How are you feeling?" he asked.

"Okay," I whispered, suddenly overcome with so much emotion.

"Okay?" he asked.

Tears trembled in my eyes, and I let out a low sob. I placed a hand over my mouth in a weak attempt to muffle it and curled my knees to my chest. I didn't know why I was crying, and I didn't know how to stop it.

"Come here," Hector murmured, drawing me closer with an arm around my shoulders.

"I'm sorry."

"There's nothing to apologize for."

"But I'm crying." I sniffled. "And I can't stop it."

He rubbed circles on my bare hip with his opposite hand. "It was an intense scene."

Is that what this was to him? All just a sex scene?

The thought made my stomach curl and the tears burn even hotter.

Of course it was to him. He had been a dominant for probably close to twenty years. This was all normal and usual for him. There was nothing special about me or between us.

Stop being stupid, Heather.

Yet to me, it seemed like so much more than that.

Another sob escaped my mouth, and I wrapped my arms tightly around his torso, my head on his chest as I listened to his steady heartbeat. I pressed my trembling lips together and whimpered against him.

"I'm so stupid," I mumbled.

He stiffened and stopped rubbing his fingers against me. "What?"

"Nothing."

"Heather, I know you didn't just say you were stupid again."

My chin quivered even harder, and I tightened my embrace. *But I am.*

Even after I had seen that BDSM contract and read it over about ten times since last night, I'd still thought that the relationship I had with Hector was more than sexual and more than just … a contract.

"Heather," Hector said, sitting up.

Instead of sitting up with him, I slouched against his abdomen, keeping my face facing away so he couldn't see my pain. I had never had this deep of a connection with someone, but maybe that was just because he had taken my virginity.

That had to be it. I wasn't falling for my father's best friend already.

"Look at me," he ordered.

I quickly wiped away my tears with the back of my hand and turned around so my head lay in his lap. He stared down at me, his expression soft yet strong, sweet but stern, and then he tucked some hair behind my ear.

"Stop saying that," he said. "It's not true."

My chest tightened, and my lips trembled again.

"Don't do that." He drew his thumb over my lips, his eyes softening more than I had seen them and his brows knotted together. "You can cry. You can be vulnerable. But please don't call yourself stupid."

"But I am."

For thinking that anything more could happen between us.

After a long pause and what looked to be Hector struggling with something internally—or maybe I was just seeing things through my tears again—Hector tilted his head a couple of centimeters to the side and brushed his thumb across my cheek.

"Why do you think that?" he asked.

I pressed my lips together.

"Heather," he said, "why do you think that?"

Tingles ran up and down my arms. The thought of saying something like that out loud to my father's best friend, knowing that this could never be anything more than just sex *because* he was my father's best friend, made bile rise in my throat.

"Please, don't make me say it out loud," I whispered.

Hector stared down at me and waited with so much patience.

More patience than Dad had for me. More patience than Eric had for me. And even more patience than Aaron had for me. Most days, I thought too slowly for them. I couldn't keep up or get my words out right.

But Hector made me feel like I could take all the time I needed.

Which only made this hurt worse.

"Hector …"

"What's wrong, sweetheart?" he asked.

Fuck, why is he so nice to me? Why can't he be a dick so I don't catch feelings?!

"Why do you think that about yourself?"

"Because I failed that stupid test."

It was a great excuse. A *perfect* excuse.

I had broken down in front of him before for that. He'd believe me this time too.

Stiffening again, Hector pulled me up into his lap so we sat face-to-face.

"If we're going to make this work, then you can't lie to me," he said.

"What do you mean, *this*?" I asked.

"Us."

"Us as in ..." I gestured around the room. "As in this us?"

Hector paused. "Yes."

With my lips pressed together, I stared at him through eyes filled with tears. I wanted him to take it all back and to tell me that he didn't mean it, that he was just messing around, and that he really meant the *us* that was more than just sex.

"I'm not lying," I said quietly when he didn't take it back.

His gaze dropped. "So, you were thinking about your professor during our scene?"

My skin crawled. "No."

He grasped my chin. "Then, what is it?"

"Nothing." I rested my forehead against his and closed my eyes. "It's nothing, Hector."

"Did I do something to make you think that?" he asked suddenly, grasping me tightly. "Because I apologize if I did. I ... I know what it feels like for someone to put you down, and ..." He paused. "And I never want to make you feel that way."

My eyes widened slightly, and I stared into his shallow gaze.

He looked to be distant from me right now, lost in his thoughts ... or his worries.

I gently cupped his face in my hands. "Who made you feel stupid?"

Because I was going to give them a piece of my mind.

After swallowing back what I assumed were memories, Hector shook his head. "That doesn't matter, Heather." He pulled me tighter to him and stared into my eyes like I meant the fucking world to him. "How can I make you feel better about yourself?"

How could I tell him that the only way to do that was to be more with me?

All he wanted was a sexual relationship.

"You can't," I whispered, wrapping my arms around his shoulders and hugging him. "It's something that I need to fix myself."

TWENTY-TWO

HECTOR

"WHAT DO I SMELL?" Heather asked, padding out into my living room.

After Radiant last night, I had brought her back to my place to calm down. She had started crying, and while I attributed it to the intensity of the scene, I didn't want her to go home like that. I'd wanted to ensure she was okay and safe.

"Breakfast," I hummed over the hot pans of eggs and home fries.

She walked over to me and tucked her head underneath my arm so she could see. "You made this?"

My lips curled into a small smile. "Yes."

"I'm surprised," she said. "Usually, guys as rich as you hire a full-time cook."

A laugh bubbled up my chest. "You think I'm lying to you?"

Her cheeks rounded, and she stared up at me with those playful eyes. "No."

After she sat at the table, I set a plate in front of her.

"Where did you learn to cook?" she asked.

"My mom."

I rarely ever cooked for anyone anymore. But when Mom had still been alive, I'd make us dinner every Monday and Friday and all the holidays too. But I hadn't done that in over a year now since she'd passed.

Halfway through breakfast, I opened the laptop that sat in the center of the dining room table and pushed it toward her. "I have something else for you to do this morning while you eat, before class."

Heather arched a brow at it and finished chewing. "So, you made me breakfast to soften the blow of forcing me to code."

While I shook my head, a low chuckle drifted from my mouth because only Heather would think something as crazy as that. Since I had woken up this morning, I had been brushing up on my coding skills. Steven knew way more about coding than I ever did, but I knew the basics. And from what I could gather, Heather had been taking a basic coding course.

"I made you breakfast because I enjoy cooking," I said. "But I'm going to force you to practice because you asked me to help you."

"I do want you to help, but …" She trailed off, staring at the code on the computer.

I gritted my teeth because I knew Heather well enough now to know that whenever she trailed off like that, she was about to say something self-deprecating, like her infamous, "I'm stupid," line. And if I heard that come out of her mouth one more time, I'd be the one to throw a fit.

"But what?"

She shrugged her shoulders. "It hurts my head, looking at it."

"Well, you have to pass, don't you?"

After grumbling to herself because she'd probably thought I would let her get out of this one, she pulled the laptop closer to her plate and ate while she attempted to fix the code I had purposefully ruined for her and asked her to find a way to download files from the laptop.

———

Forty minutes later, Heather slid the computer across the table and jumped up. "I tried. And if I don't leave now, then I'm going to be late for his stupid class." After she tugged on her coat, she paused in front of me, her gaze drifting down to my lips. "I will, uh, see you tonight at Radiant."

She twirled around to head back toward the door, but before she could leave, I snaked my hand behind her neck and pulled her into a kiss.

She sucked in a sharp breath and placed her hands on my abdomen, relaxing underneath my touch. After gently kissing me back, she pulled away and wiped her lips, a giggle escaping her mouth.

"I'll see you later," she said, tucking some hair behind her ear.

"See you tonight."

Bouncing on her toes, she headed for the door and pulled it open. "Oh."

I glanced up to see Steven standing at my door with a huge box and about to knock.

After Heather slipped past him, Steven leaned against the doorway and nodded his head toward her retreating figure. "Uh, I was not expecting to see someone at your house so early in the morning."

"What are you doing here?" I asked.

"Michelle sent me to deliver some … *goods* to your home."

Eyes rolling, I grabbed the box from his hands and glanced inside to see about a hundred floppy dildos just sitting casually inside it. I ran a hand over my face and set the box on my dining room table.

"Curse that woman," I mumbled underneath my breath.

I tell her not to give me any more toys, and she sends a box of them.

"Anyway, perfect timing," I hummed, walking over to the computer. "Can you look something over for me?"

"What is this?"

"Code."

Steven arched a brow. "You sound like Michelle with that sarcastic answer."

"Heather failed her last exam in one of her classes and wanted me to help her study. I gave her some instructions this morning to fix some code. And"—I looked down at it and ran it to see if the code succeeded—"it works."

Steven chuckled. "Is that a bad thing?"

"No, but she said she failed her most recent exam on this stuff. I'm just confused."

After setting his coat on the back of the chair, Steven sat down and pulled the laptop toward him, scrolling down the page and scanning the code. "Hector, this is Java, one of the harder languages to understand for students new to software engineering."

"And?"

"And it looks like code written by someone with ten years of experience."

My eyes widened. "Really?"

"It's modular." He looked up at me. "Did she search up the answer?"

"Not for this," I said. "For her exam, she said that she had access to the internet."

Steven pushed the laptop to the center of the table. "I don't know what happened with her exam, but this code is better than the code that some software engineers that I've hired produced."

"Interesting," I hummed, drawing my tongue across my teeth.

Either Heather wasn't great at taking exams or her professor had failed her on purpose.

While I had seen Heather under pressure before—and albeit she didn't do well while stressed—I doubted that it was just a coincidence that she had flunked last year and was failing this year with the same professor.

And I was going to get to the bottom of it.

CHAPTER
TWENTY-THREE

HEATHER

"SOOOO," Sierra said, kicking her legs back and forth underneath the table at Carnegie Coffee Company. She flipped through her textbook aimlessly, her gaze on me and her smirk contagious. "How was your night with Daddy's BFF?"

"Good."

"Just good?"

"Sorry. It was fucking fabulous," I clarified. "But I feel like I totally fucked it up."

"How?"

"After we had sex, I burst out crying."

Sierra's eyes widened. "Oh."

My lips turned into a frown, and I glanced over my shoulder at Mom, who walked into the coffee shop. She was supposed to meet up to go over the contract with me. After smiling at us, she headed to the counter.

So, I leaned forward and lowered my voice. "We're never going to be together."

"You don't know that," Sierra said.

"Come on," I explained. "He's my father's best friend."

"So?"

"So?!"

"Steven is my professor."

"Your sex ed professor," I said. "Plus, that's different."

Sierra crossed her arms on top of her textbook and leaned closer. "How?"

"Because he doesn't know any of your family," I said, the words slipping out of my mouth before I could stop them. A few years ago, Sierra's entire family had died in a car accident right before Christmas. I sighed and grabbed her hand. "Sorry, I didn't mean it like that."

"It's okay, Heather." She smiled softly, though it didn't meet her eyes. "I know."

My frown deepened, chest tightening. I hated making Sierra reminisce about her family.

"Oh, girls," Mom called from the counter, picking up some napkins. "I got your favorites!"

When Sierra and I had moved into the same dorm our freshman year of college and I found out what had happened to her family, my parents had immediately taken her in and treated her like their own. And while Sierra hated taking anything from anyone, I thought she'd grown fond of Mom.

Sierra giggled beside me, watching Mom waltz over after throwing some businessman a seductive smirk.

"I can't believe you asked your mom to look over the BDSM contract." She snickered. "My parents would have killed me if they found out that I was attending a BDSM club, never mind sleeping with an older man."

"Shush!" I said, playfully pushing her away. "She doesn't know about Hector."

"Sweetheart," Mom said, handing Sierra a cup, "here's your tea."

"Thank you," Sierra said shyly. "You didn't have to do that."

"Nonsense." Mom sat down. "Heather, yours should be finished soon too. Now ..." After setting her purse on the empty chair beside her, she pulled out the contract and set it in front of me. "I don't have any revisions. It is heavily in your favor. And you can terminate the contract whenever you'd like with no repercussions."

I rummaged through my backpack for a pen and flipped to the last sheet.

Before I signed, Mom grabbed my wrist. "Do you have any questions about it?"

"Nope. Hec—*he* explained pretty much all of it to me."

When Mom released my wrist, I placed the pen on the line and signed my life away. If I could be with Hector, even for a few months, maybe a year or so, and we could do it behind Dad's back, then I wanted it.

As much as it'd break my heart when we were finished …

"So, who's it with?" Mom turned to Sierra. "Do you know?"

"Mom!" I exclaimed. "I already told you that I can't tell you."

"It is totally someone that I know, isn't it?"

"No."

"Someone that comes to the Christmas parties?"

"Mom!"

Mom giggled. "Oh, it's definitely someone who will piss your father off."

My cheeks burned with embarrassment, and I shoved the contract into my backpack. "It is definitely nobody who comes over to the Christmas parties …" Though it one hundred percent was someone who came over for more than just a couple of parties.

Mom just couldn't know that.

While my parents weren't together anymore, they still talked. And I would much rather them *not* talk about who I was dating. They could rave about my brother all they wanted, but as soon as Hector and I came out of their mouths …

I would die. Literally die.

When Mom began asking Sierra about her sex life—because Mom loved all the tea and gossip—I pulled out my phone and scrolled to Hector's contact, my core growing warm at all the dirty messages that he had sent me today.

Me: When I sign the contract, am I officially your submissive?

Three little bubbles appeared on the screen, and then a message came through.

Hector: Yes.

Warmth spread throughout my body, and I pressed my thighs together discreetly underneath the table.

Me: Well then, I'll see you in a couple of hours, Sir. 😏

TWENTY-FOUR

HEATHER

TWO HOURS LATER, I shuffled through the doors at Radiant and headed straight for the restroom to put on something a bit … sexier than I had on now. After Mom had left the coffee shop earlier, I had bought a fitted dress at a sex shop and decided to surprise Hector.

As his submissive for the first time.

I leaned across the counter in the restroom, applying some mascara.

Would he go easy on me because I'd signed his contract even if I was a brat? Or would he be even stricter with his punishments, forcing me to crawl around Radiant in this dress, my drooling pussy on display while I asked other Doms about what kind of punishment Hector should give me tonight?

Warmth spread through my body, and I pressed my thighs together.

Hector could never find out how hot I thought all his punishments really were.

Because he'd take them all away.

After the toilet flushed, someone opened the stall door behind me. I glanced in the mirror to catch Evelyn heading toward the sinks where I stood.

When she saw me, she stopped in her tracks and widened her eyes. "Heather, I—"

I placed my mascara down and twisted my head. "Please, don't tell me my dad is here."

She placed her purse on the counter. "Maybe."

"Hector and I—I mean …" I started, scratching the back of my head.

Oh shit. Why'd I let that slip?

"I know you're sleeping with him," she said. "It's okay."

My eyes widened, and I grabbed her hand. "Please, don't tell my father."

She paused for a moment, then giggled. "Don't worry. I won't."

Eyeing her for a few moments, I slumped my shoulders forward and blew out a breath that I had been holding since I had seen her in here. "How'd you find out about us anyway? Did he tell you?"

"At the office, it was kinda obvious when your father stepped out of the room."

"Oh."

Stupid me for forgetting that she had basically watched him scold me the other day for not coming to Radiant. I wondered what else she had seen. Had she been watching the entire time? Maybe she'd heard me crying his name after he tied me up.

"Are you going to see him tonight?" she asked in an attempt at small talk.

"Yes."

After washing and drying her hands, she pulled out some bright red lipstick from her purse and tilted her head toward me. "Here." She swiped it across my lips. "Not that you need it, but I've always thought this color would look hot on you."

My eyes widened slightly. "You … what?"

"I've always thought it'd look sexy on you," she repeated.

An awkward—or maybe I was just making it awkward—silence fell upon us.

Then, she cleared her throat. "So, um, about your dad and me …"

"I won't say anything to him about me knowing about you two as long as you don't say anything to him about Hector and me," I said, extending my arm and holding out my hand, as if we were making some business transaction.

"Deal." She giggled. "You know, you're nicer than I thought you'd be."

I turned toward the mirror and rubbed my lips together. "Oh God, what, do I look like a bitch?"

"No, but I've mostly been jealous of you," she said, tucking some hair behind her ear. Her diamond earrings looked like a gift that Dad had definitely picked out for her. "When I got hired, I had a major crush on your dad."

I scrunched my nose. "Ew."

"At first, I thought he liked you because he talked about you all the time—and still does. And you're so pretty." Another giggle. "But then I found out you were his daughter, and I was so embarrassed."

"Oh, stop it," I said, playfully pushing her away. "You literally look like a beauty influencer."

But I couldn't get past the fact that … Dad talked about me. And if Evelyn had been jealous of the way he did talk about me, then it must've been all good, right? But that didn't make sense, as he was *always* making me feel … lesser.

Or maybe that was just the way I thought he treated me … the way I felt when comparing myself to my brother …

After Evelyn grabbed her purse, she headed for the door. "I'll try to convince your dad to leave, but we just got here. And I'm not sure he's going to want to go anytime soon." She glanced over her shoulder. "But I'll try."

Once she slipped out of the restroom, I leaned against the counter and smiled softly at the closed door. I never thought that I would ever like Evelyn because her looks were so damn intimidating, but she seemed sweet.

After pausing for a few more minutes in the restroom to give her time to convince Dad to leave, I snuck out of the restroom and tiptoed down the hallway, glancing around the doorway to see into the main room.

Someone slapped a hand over my mouth and yanked me into a dark hallway.

"Don't say a word," Hector whispered into my ear. "Your father is still here."

I glanced around the doorway and spotted Dad sitting with a bunch of other men I recognized from Hector's company and then pulled my head back into the hallway so he wouldn't see me.

"How are we going to get upstairs?" I asked.

Hector pressed against me from behind, grinding his dick on my ass. "We're not."

CHAPTER
TWENTY-FIVE

HEATHER

AFTER FLIPPING up the back of my dress, Hector ground his bulge against me and grunted into my ear, "This dress looks so fucking amazing on you." His warm breath fanned my neck, his lips pressing against my nape.

I pressed my fingers into the wall and peered into the main room.

What were we doing?!

Anyone could walk out from the restrooms behind us or step into this small hallway from the main room, and if they did … then we would have nowhere to go. Nowhere to hide. They'd find us here with Hector's cock buried inside me.

But, hell, I didn't want to stop.

Not now.

"Why don't you take it off me?" I purred.

"Heather," he growled.

"What?" I hummed, warmth exploding between my thighs. "Are you too afraid that—"

Hector ripped the zipper down and shoved the dress to my ankles, leaving me completely naked in this small hallway. I arched my back, the pleasure already coursing through my body from his dick against my ass.

He yanked off his tie, pulled my hands above my head, and bound my wrists together. I leaned forward, my breasts pressing against the wall while my ass was nearly a foot from it, grinding up and down on his huge bulge.

"If your father sees us …" he murmured, clicking his tongue.

"He won't."

I didn't know why I was so sure, but there was no going back now. I was in the middle of Hector's sex club, naked and with his tie binding my wrists together. If Dad walked back here and saw us, we'd both be screwed.

But that wouldn't stop me from being Hector's submissive.

The contract was signed.

He grasped my hips and pulled them further back, his fingers sweeping in circles around my bare skin. His lips moved lower on my neck, around my shoulders, and down my spine. "I'm going to make your ass red."

A moment after his lips met my hip, he slapped my ass cheeks hard. I yelped out, my body jerking forward and my tits bouncing against the wall. He sprawled a hand over my lower back to steady me, then spanked me again.

"You know not to back-talk me," he said. "Remember what happened last time."

Warmth spread through my body, and my nipples hardened. "Why don't you remind—"

After another hard slap, he wrapped a hand around the front of my neck and yanked me back toward him, his mouth on my ear. "I'm sure you don't want me to hold your orgasms from you again. Now, spread your legs and take my dick like a good girl."

Biting back a moan, I pressed my thighs together.

Hector growled into my ear, "Spread. Your. Legs."

"Make me."

He chuckled darkly behind me. "You don't want to do this, Heather."

"Don't tell me what I do and don't wa—"

Before I could finish my sentence, he slapped my ass hard again and pulled my upper body off the wall with his grip on my neck. I still pressed my thighs together, my cunt aching and drooling in anticipation.

After forcing his free hand between my thighs, he cupped my pussy and pressed his fingers against my clit. I sucked in a sharp breath, shoving my thighs even harder together, yet Hector slipped his fingers inside me instead.

"You're going to regret this," he growled against my shoulder.

"I don't think I'm going to regret anything, Hector. I think you're going to lose control and fuck me like you've been aching to do all day," I said, a moan escaping my lips as he pumped his fingers in and out of me. "I think you're going to dump all of your cum—"

Hooking two fingers into my pussy, he tilted my head to the side and toward the door, then shoved his hips into mine, sending me stumbling forward and directly in front of the door. So, if anyone looked over … they'd see me.

Naked and bound.

"Hector!" I snapped.

Heat coursed through my body. I never—*ever*—wanted Dad to see me naked in a sex club that he apparently attended, but the thought of being caught with Hector did something to me. Something oh-so bad.

Instead of pulling me back behind the doorway, Hector slammed his fingers deeper into me. Pumping them in and out. Grinding his bulge against my bare ass. He released his grip on my neck and undid his zipper.

Within a moment, he whipped out his huge cock, bent me all the way forward so my bound wrists dangled near my ankles, and slammed into me. My tits bounced, and a loud moan escaped my mouth.

"Hector," I cried. "He's going to see."

"Apologize."

"No."

He slammed into me harder, and a louder cry escaped my mouth.

"Apologize to your Master."

"Hec—"

He grabbed a fistful of my hair and yanked it back until he could press his mouth against my ear. "If you don't apologize to me right now, I'll rip off my belt, wrap it around your pretty little throat, and walk you like a pet out into the main room."

Warmth exploded through my body, and I clenched around him.

One moment passed. Then another.

Then, suddenly, Hector pulled out of me and shoved me to my knees.

"I'm sorry," I begged. "Please don't."

He ripped off his belt and wrapped it around my neck, buckling it on the tightest hole.

I placed my bound hands on his cock and stroked him quickly, desperate for him to forgive me. My pussy was drooling all over the floor. I jerked him faster and faster, nipples aching as he yanked up on the belt.

"I'm sorry, Sir. I'm sorry. I'm sorry. I'm sorry. I'm—"

Before I could get out another word, he shoved his dick into my mouth. It slammed against the back of my throat and choked me.

"Show your Master how sorry you are for disobeying him."

I wrapped my hands around the front of my throat and squeezed around the bulge of his cock deep inside it. Through teary eyes, I stared up at him and stroked it up and down, swallowing again and again around it.

"I'm sorry," I gargled, the words muffled.

Hector groaned, his eyes rolling back and his body stiffening the way it did right before he came.

"I'm sor—"

He slammed his dick deeper down my throat as spit ran down

my chin and came inside me. After a few more thrusts and grunts, he pulled out of me. I fell forward onto my hands, and Hector crouched in front of me.

"You will learn not to be a brat," he said, picking me up. "Let's get you cleaned up."

HECTOR

WITH HEATHER'S head on my chest, I gently moved my fingertips up and down her upper arm. I didn't know how her father hadn't seen us sneak through the main room together after our sexcapade in the hallway.

"I might or might not have something for you," Heather said, looking up at me.

"Is that so?" I hummed.

After she slipped out of my hold, she scurried out of the bed and found her bag on the dresser. She rummaged through it, tossing out some dirty clothes and grabbing a stack of papers and a pen.

She sashayed back over, naked and so goddamn pretty under the dim light. I turned onto my side and propped my head up on my hand as she sat beside me, draping my arm around her waist.

I looked over her hips to see her flipping through the contract that I had given her, expecting her to have revisions about it. But when she made it to the last page and I spotted her signature on the line, my eyes widened.

"Does this make me your submissive?" she asked, giddy.

I snatched the pen from her and immediately signed the line beside hers. "Now, it does."

Her mouth dropped open. "You didn't even read it over."

"I don't need to," I said because I would've done anything for her to be my submissive.

"What if I made a revision to it?"

"It wouldn't matter."

"What if I forced you to sell me your entire company? Or to, like, give me all your money?"

I tilted my head a couple of centimeters to the side and smiled. "I trust you."

"You shouldn't," she hummed. "I'm a brat."

"You're a brat," I said. "Not a bitch."

She opened and closed her mouth a handful of times, then peered back at my signature. "I've just never seen anyone sign a contract that quickly, especially you. You and my dad go back and forth on contracts for days. Weeks. Why did you sign it so quickly?"

My lips curled into a small smile, a warmth spreading through my chest. "Because."

Those pretty eyes stared down at me, telling me she wasn't taking that as an answer.

"Because why?" she asked.

"Why'd *you* sign it so quickly?" I asked. "You were so eager."

After crossing her arms over her chest, she smirked. "*Because.*"

A few quiet moments passed between us, and I hoped that she had signed the contract eagerly and quickly because she felt the same way I did about her. But her bratty little mouth would never admit something like that if I didn't first.

So, I pulled her down to lie with me. "Have you spoken to your professor?"

She stiffened. "About what? The test?"

"Yes."

"Why?" she asked, chewing on her cheek. "Was my code that bad?"

"No." I buried my face into the crook of her neck. "Steven said it was flawless."

"What?" she asked.

"Have you talked to him?"

"Yes," she said, voice barely above a whisper. "He said that there was nothing I can do."

I arched a brow. "Are you lying to me?"

She sucked in her inner cheek. "No …"

"That's an awfully drawn-out response."

After sighing, she looked over at me, hair a mess on the pillows. "Fine, I did. But there's nothing I can do about it."

"Nothing?"

"Nothing."

She fumbled with her fingers, then turned on her side to face me. I tucked a strand of hair behind her ear.

"He did say that I could do something, but I hate him, so it's not happening. I'm not going to stoop that low."

"What'd he say?"

When she *still* didn't want to tell me, I pulled my head back slightly and looked over at her. If he'd asked her to do *anything* inappropriate after failing her for perfect goddamn code, then I would do more than get him fired from the university.

"Tell me," I said softly. "What'd he say?"

"He said that he'd give me a good grade if I could get him an interview at your company. Don't worry—"

"Deal."

"What?"

"I'll let him interview with the company."

"Are you kidding me?!" She sat up. "You're really going to give him an interview?"

I pulled her back to me. "Yes."

"That asshole doesn't deserve it. I would rather fail his class three times over."

"Well, I'm not going to let that happen."

He would have an interview with me next week. Not because

he would ever get a job at my company. Because I wanted to embarrass that dickhead so hard in front of Heather that he walked out of my office with his pants pissed and all of Heather's grades corrected.

"Hector, you don't have to do that for me," she said. "We can—"

"Next Monday at three p.m." My lips curled into a smirk. "Tell him not to be late."

HEATHER

SATURDAY MORNING, I walked through the busy mall in Robinson with Hector holding a few bags of designer clothes for me.

"What are you smiling about?" I asked, glancing over at him.

This might or might not have been the first time we were out where a bunch of people could see us, together and sorta like a date. Okay, it definitely wasn't a date … maybe … but apparently, it'd become a shopping spree for Hector.

To get me clothes.

"Nothing," he hummed, spotting another upscale boutique. "Come on."

"Hector"—I stumbled after him—"do you think being out and about on a Saturday is—"

"I fucked you while you were naked at my club with your father in the other room," Hector said, louder than he should've. A couple of people glanced over at us. "I think going out with you on a busy Saturday will be fine."

A pretty, young personal shopper approached us, but Hector walked right by her without a second look and headed straight for the women's section. From what I'd gathered, Hector enjoyed the old-money look, like something you'd find straight out of the beaches of New England in the summer.

I smiled at the woman so she wouldn't completely despise us and followed Hector. He found a couple of simple pieces of clothing that could be worn on almost any occasion besides formal or black-tie events and then headed to the fitting room.

While I shuffled into the first outfit, I glanced into the mirror to see Hector.

"I expected you to have your mother revise the contract," he said when we made eye contact, sitting in a suede chair in the corner of the changing room with a smirk on his face. "But I looked it over last night, and there wasn't anything changed."

"Should there have been?" I asked.

"No."

After tugging on a white button-up that cost about one hundred sixty dollars, I twirled around and faced him, brow arched. "Why is that smirk still on your face?" I asked, hands on my hips. "What is it?"

"You did read the contract, didn't you?"

"Yes, we read it together."

"And there wasn't anything that you wanted changed?"

I pressed my lips together, thinking back to when he had caught me reading the contract. I swore I had read everything over, and it had looked completely fine at the time. Hell, even Mom had read it over and thought it was—

"Oh no," I whispered, eyes widening.

"Heather, Heather, Heather." He stood and stalked over to me, his hand capturing my chin and lifting so I looked up at him. He drew a single finger down my chest and between my breasts. "You're my full-time submissive."

My throat dried. *How did I miss that?!*

"Do you know what that means?" he asked.

"That I'm yours whenever you'd like," I whispered.

"It means that you have the expectation"—he moved closer, so his lips were millimeters away from mine—"to live at my home with me, to let me purchase your clothes and anything that you might need, to let me take care of you."

While I might be freaking out on the inside, I decided to play it off.

"Sounds like *someone* wants me to depend on him so I can't leave."

He stiffened a bit, then let out a small chuckle. "You're right."

My eyes widened. "What?"

"I want you to depend on me," he said, drawing his finger back up my chest, up my neck, and to my chin. "The moment you signed our contract, you became mine. And if you're my girl, then I'm going to give you everything that you need."

If I was his *girl* … not his submissive.

While I didn't have a problem taking Dad's money because he had spoiled me since I had been a little girl, I felt a little guilty about taking Hector's money to pay for all my clothes. But if he was going to hold the whole full-time submissive over my head …

Then I planned to use all the benefits that came with it.

I gulped down my fear and met his intense stare.

Full-time submissive.

If he had known since last night, then why hadn't he asked me to do *anything* yet? No sex. No blow jobs. No crawling around his high-rise naked. Heck, he'd even made me breakfast this morning, and we had eaten on his private balcony.

Mom had said that I could terminate the contract whenever I wanted, but maybe it wouldn't be so bad being Hector Patton's full-time submissive. Maybe if I did, I could earn myself a collar and be his for longer than either of us expected …

CHAPTER
TWENTY-EIGHT

HEATHER

FRIDAY MORNING, I stood in the middle of Hector and Dad's main office and stared at the elevators. My heart was racing about a hundred miles a minute, and I couldn't get it to stop. Today was the day that Professor Eric had an interview.

In twelve minutes, to be exact.

And Hector wasn't here yet.

I grabbed my phone from my purse and texted my group chat with the girls.

Me: I'M FREAKING OUT! SEND HELP.

Suddenly, the elevator chimed. My gaze snapped up to it, and I spotted Hector stepped out of the small compartment. Brunette hair pulled up into a high ponytail, Evelyn walked out of the elevator with a short pencil skirt and a low-cut fuchsia top.

They were talking quietly to each other, and they were close … so close. He had told me not to worry about Evelyn, and she had even seemed so nice at Radiant—plus, she was banging my dad— but still … I didn't feel like I could compare.

After she nodded to him, he headed to his office while she walked my way.

"Morning, Heather." She beamed.

I chewed on the inside of my cheek. "Morning. What were you and, uh …"

Fuck, that sounded like me being a jealous bitch.

"Hector and I were talking about?" she finished. "Just something for later."

"Oh."

She smiled. "Don't worry about it. I'm not into him like I am with your fa—"

"Okay! Okay! I don't need the details!" I said, my phone beginning to buzz like crazy.

Because … ew.

"What're you up to?" she asked, grabbing some papers off her desk.

"Oh, uh …" I said, smoothing out my shirt. "Just waiting for Hector to start an interview."

For some reason, her smile widened. "I heard. You going to *help* him out during it?"

I arched a brow, a giggle bubbling up in my throat. "No, not like that!"

"Evelyn!" Dad shouted from his office. "I need you in here."

After Evelyn winked at me, I swallowed some bile that rose in my throat from the thought of her doing *that* with my father and pulled out my phone to check the group chat, which was on fire right now, just to calm my nerves.

Sun: What happened??

Athena: Heather???

Athena: What's going on?

Sierra: Her professor has a job interview at her dad's company.

Sierra: She's nervous about it …

Sierra: And maybe being dramatic.

Um, excuse me, Sierra, Miss Insecure About Everything!

Me: I'm not being dramatic! This is serious!

Sun: What time is the interview?

Me: Five minutes!
Sun: Who is doing the interview?
Sierra: Hector.
Athena: Oh. 🤣🤣 I thought this was actually something serious.

My eyes widened, and I began pacing the floor, almost bumping into everyone.

Me: This is serious!
Athena: It's literally an interview with the guy you're dating.
Sierra: You think Hector's actually going to give him the job?
Athena: No!
Sun: I don't know. He seems to really like her.
Athena: Exactly why he's not going to give him the job.
Athena: He's probably going to just put him in his place.
Athena: Ya know, embarrass him. 😌

I chewed on the inside of my cheek and stared at Hector's office door. While Evelyn was doing God knew what with Dad to keep him distracted, Hector had asked me to come in today to oversee his interview with Eric, and I was having *NONE* of this!

All I wanted was to crawl back into my bed and cry myself to sleep because Hector had actually decided to give that asshole an interview. I needed to pass, but not this badly. I should've never opened my big mouth.

Between begging to give him blow jobs all day and promising to never be a brat again, I had pleaded with him to not let me come today. I didn't want to watch him give a job to a man that I hated just to get me a good grade in the class.

In fact, I would do close to anything to get out of it.

Athena: You're going to be fine.
Athena: He's not getting the job!
Me: You don't know that!
Me: If he does, then I'm going to have to see his face even more during the week.
Me: I will literally throw up if that happens. 🤢🤮
Sierra: Drama 🙄 hehe

The elevator dinged, and I shoved my phone into my pocket, squeezed my eyes closed, and whined. Why was this happening to me?! Why was this happening to me?! Why was this happening to meeee?

When I reopened my eyes, Professor fucking Eric stepped out of the elevator. His hair was greased back like a wannabe gangster. He had on a suit that looked way too big for him. And this goddamn man was looking straight at me.

Me!

With a smirk!

"Head up, Heather," Hector hummed from his door. "You shouldn't be slouching, nor signing. I might need to teach you proper etiquette later this evening." After tsking and shaking his head at me, Hector walked right to the elevator doors to greet that stupid piece-of-shit professor that shouldn't be teaching in the first place. "Eric, I'm Hector. It's nice to meet you."

TWENTY-NINE

HECTOR

I SHOOK Eric's hand and placed a hand on his shoulder, squeezing lightly, like I would to an old friend to make him feel comfortable, to get him to trust me, to like me before I cut him down and burned him in front of Heather.

"Eric, I've been so excited to chat with you," I said.

Eric shook my hand stronger than I'd expected his scrawny ass to and smirked over at Heather, staring at her for much longer than I was comfortable with. He liked her. There wasn't a doubt in my mind that he had been failing her purposefully to get closer to her.

To try to fuck her. Blackmail her.

"All thanks to Heather," he said, his gaze dropping down her body for a moment.

A damn moment, but I had seen it.

"Come on into my office," I said, extending my arm to show him the way.

He headed through the main office like he already worked here and walked into my personal office off the main floor and next to our executive conference room.

When I walked past Heather, I hummed, "You too."

She frowned, trudged in behind us, and shut the door.

I pulled out a seat across from me for Heather, but that asshole sat down first. I clenched my teeth lightly and pulled out the chair beside him for her. When she sat, she shot me a glare because she didn't know what I was planning.

"Well, Eric"—I sat across from him—"why don't you tell me a bit about yourself?"

"I've been working at the university for three years now and have had the honor of having Heather as a student for two semesters. I'm looking to pursue more of a career with software engineers who actually know what they're doing."

"Ah, yes," I said. "Teaching students must be hard."

Especially when you purposefully fail them when they should be succeeding in your class …

"Like you wouldn't believe." He chuckled.

"Oh, I believe it." I drew my tongue across my teeth and tried to keep my composure, but Heather's face was red with fury, which pissed me off even more for her. "Must be distracting, too, with all those pretty girls who'd do anything to get a passing grade."

Her anger would be worth it in the end.

"Some do …" His eyes flickered to Heather. "Others … not so much."

"Your résumé looks very impressive," I praised, glancing over at Heather, who sat with her arms crossed and a scowl on her face, not once peeking over at Eric. "And Heather has told me so many good things about you."

Of course, it was a lie. But I wanted to build him up, to make him feel like he was on top of the world. Humiliation always hit harder that way. I had learned that from the years and years of abuse back at home, before getting adopted.

He smiled at her. "I'm glad to hear that."

"Well …" I pulled my desk open and grabbed two laptops. "I thought we could start with you showing me some of your skills.

This test is what we give to all our developers during an interview. I was thinking it'd be fun for Heather to do it alongside you so she could brush up on her skills and maybe … *learn* from you."

Heather's glare intensified as I set the laptop in front of her.

The test used a coding language that not many developers could read, but Eric had written on his résumé that he was familiar with it. And because I didn't like the asshole, I'd had Steven create a pile of hot garbage code that wasn't usable as it was.

You know … just to give it to Eric to fix.

"Sounds great!" Eric said. "I'm sure she'll learn something."

———

"Having trouble?" I hummed after he had stared at the screen for fifteen minutes, typing a bunch and then erasing it all. Over and over and over. Until Heather's lips actually turned up into the smallest of smiles, the way they did before she was about to giggle.

"No, sir. I just need a couple more minutes."

"It can't be that hard," I said. "Heather's already done with the first question."

"Actually," Heather whispered, "I'm finished with it all."

My lips curled into a smile. *Even better.*

Eric shot his gaze over to her. "Impossible."

I stood up and walked around my desk to the laptop that I had set in front of him. "How many years of work experience did you say you had again?" I tilted the laptop toward Heather and gripped that asshole's shoulder. "Why don't you give him a jump-start, sweetheart? Looks like he needs it."

"I don't need it," he growled, yanking the computer back. "Just give me a minute."

After releasing his shoulder from my grasp, I walked back to my seat and leaned back in it. "It must be quite embarrassing to have one of your own failing students complete an entire test before you can even get through the first question, huh?"

Eric stared down at the laptop, his ears growing red and his teeth gritted.

"Why do you think I would ever hire someone as incompetent as you?" I asked him. "Why would I lower my company's standards to fit your capabilities if you can't find a solution to a single problem that one of your students—"

Suddenly, Eric stood and slammed his hands on my desk. "I see where your stupid daughter gets her mouth from. I'm not going to sit here and be belittled by the CEO of a company that I never wanted to have an interview at in the first place."

"Oh, Heather isn't my daughter," I said, lips turning into a grin. "She's my submissive."

Eric's eyes grew wider, angrier.

I kept my gaze steady. "And it's my job to keep her safe from dickheads like you."

After seething for a few more moments, he abruptly grabbed his coat, stormed to my office door, and tried to pull it open. He yanked on it again and again, but it wouldn't budge. Not even an inch.

"Ah, I forgot to mention. I asked one of our lovely assistants, Evelyn, to lock the door when your interview began, just in case something like this happened." I stood up to meet his glare. "So, if I were you, I would come back to your seat and start begging."

"Start begging for what?" he spat. "What're you going to do to me?"

"That's something you don't want to find out, Eric." My lips curled into a smirk. "*Really*. Because if you think me humiliating you in front of Heather was bad, wait until the board finds out that you flunked one of your students and tried to blackmail her. So … *start begging*."

A flurry of emotions rushed over Eric's face, finally landing on panic. "You wouldn't."

"I would."

He looked over at Heather. "He—"

Before he could say another word to her, I was standing in front of him, snapping his chin in my hand and forcing him to look at me. "You will only speak to her if you're going to apologize and beg for her forgiveness. And even then, you're not going to look her in the eye. You'll sit on your knees with your head bowed. Submissive to her."

CHAPTER
THIRTY

"BEG," Hector growled, stepping away from Eric. "Beg for her forgiveness."

My mouth hung open, and I stared at Hector through wide eyes. Evelyn had mentioned that Eric would never get the job and that Hector would embarrass him, but I had not even a little bit expected *this*!

Eric hung his head. "I'm sorry, Heather."

Hector grabbed his collar. "I said, on your knees."

When Hector released him, Eric went flying down to the floor and landed on his knees with a thud. He stared down at the ground and shook his head. "You're not … you can't do this to me. I'll sue you for—"

"I don't care what you'll try to sue me for," Hector growled. "All it takes is one phone call, and I will ruin the rest of your pathetic life."

Heat rushed through me, and I found this oddly … satisfying.

After opening and closing his mouth a handful of times, Eric finally sat back on his heels. He lifted his gaze to the windows, his expression looking as if he was going through all the possibilities about how this could end in his head.

"I'm not going to fucking say it again," Hector snarled. "Beg."

"I'm sorry," Eric whispered. "I'm sorry for flunking you."

"You beg her at her feet," Hector said. "Crawl to her like a fucking dog."

Eyes widening, I looked up at Hector, who showed absolutely no sign of backing down or stopping. He actually didn't care if Eric sued him or not—and for what … I didn't know. Hector was dead set on humiliating him more than he had with me.

To my surprise, Eric began crawling from the door to Hector's desk on his hands and knees. His tie dangled to the ground, and his eyes were averted from my and Hector's gaze at all times. And once he reached me, he sat back on his heels.

Head bowed.

"I'm sorry, Heather."

"Louder," Hector commanded.

"I'm sorry, Heather."

"Louder."

"I'm sorry, Heather!" Eric said. "I'm sorry for failing you. I should've never done it."

After a few moments of silence, Eric looked up at Hector. "Is that good enough for you? Is that what you wanted to hear from me? That I failed her purposefully? That I apologize for what I did?"

Hector looked at me. "Sweetheart, does his apology make up for the past twelve months of your life that he's wasted?"

Heart pounding inside my chest, I looked from Hector to Eric, then back to Hector. I opened my mouth, but no words would come out, no matter how hard I tried. I probably looked so stupid, sitting with my mouth open, but I was speechless that this was even happening.

"Does his apology make up for what he's done to you?" Hector asked again.

My throat was dry, but I still swallowed. "No."

"Do you hear that, Eric?" Hector crouched beside him. "You're not begging loud enough."

"Please," Eric said louder, more desperately, his head bowed again and now shaking sporadically. "Please, forgive me, Heather. All I wanted was for you to stay after with me. If you had asked for extra credit, I would've … given you all of it."

I sat up taller in my seat. "I did ask you for extra credit."

But he … must've meant the non-moral kind. The corrupt kind.

Fury rose inside me, and I clenched my fists. The more and more I thought about it, maybe he really did want to sleep with me. Maybe him asking for an interview had been a last-minute decision when I called him out for his gross ways.

"That's not enough," I whispered, slowly standing. "This isn't enough."

Hector reached across his desk and handed me a marker. At first, I didn't know what he wanted me to do with it, but my body seemed to know exactly what *I* wanted to do with it. I knew exactly how to make this a little bit better.

"You're going to resign," I said, "so you don't do this to anyone ever again."

"B-but …"

"You're going to resign," Hector commanded. "You'll do as she wishes."

"Okay, okay," Eric agreed. "Is that enough?"

I crouched down in front of him and grabbed his chin.

When he looked me in the eye, Hector growled, "I told you not to look at her, so drop your gaze like the submissive little prick you are."

To my surprise, Eric dropped his gaze.

Then, with a permanent marker, I wrote all over his face, all over his body, using words that I knew a man who tried to take advantage of women never wanted to be associated with. Words that would embarrass and humiliate him the same way he'd embarrassed and humiliated me. Words that he wouldn't be caught dead with in public.

Payback—my lips curled into a smirk—was a bitch.

CHAPTER
THIRTY-ONE

HECTOR

ONCE HEATHER FINISHED PAYING back Eric for all the shit he had put her through these past two semesters, I grabbed him by the collar and picked him up off the ground. I dragged his ass to the door and unlocked it.

After tossing him out into the main office, where my employees looked over, I crouched down to his level so he would know that I wasn't playing around, that I would do anything to protect Heather.

"Get out of my office," I growled at Eric. "And don't you ever come back."

Eric scrambled to his feet, piss staining the front of his pants.

Before he could run out in embarrassment, I grabbed his tie. "If Heather tells me that you *ever* reach out to her again, I will personally find a punishment that fits you. And if you pissed yourself over this, you won't like what I have in store. Understand?"

"Y-yes, s-sir!"

Everyone in the office stayed silent as he stumbled down the walkway toward the elevator, frantically pushing the down arrow.

The elevator doors beeped, and a bunch of executives walked out together.

I leaned against the door and stuffed my hands into my pockets, loving every moment of this embarrassment's life right now. Eric's face turned a darker shade of red, and he scrambled into the car.

When the doors closed, Evelyn giggled from the opposite corner of the room with her hand over her mouth.

I cleared my throat and looked at the secretaries and executives. "Get back to work." Then, I walked back into my office and closed my door.

While I expected Heather to be beaming behind me, she sat on the couch with a frown.

"What's wrong?" I asked, walking over to her and crouching beside her. I tucked some hair behind her ear and drew the pad of my thumb softly across her cheek. "He's not going to bother you ever again, Heather."

"I know," she whispered. "I just feel bad."

"Why?"

She wrapped her arms around herself. "I should've known."

"How could you have known his true intentions?" I asked.

She shrugged and glanced at the door, chewing on her inner cheek. She didn't think she was good enough, smart enough, persistent enough, even though Eric had admitted to wrongfully failing her.

And not because he wanted an interview, but because he wanted *her*.

"Come on," she said, voice smaller. "If I had known those were his intentions from the very beginning, then I could've tried to bring it up with the dean ... but I didn't pick up on it and wasted multiple semesters of my life. Sometimes, I'm just stu—"

"Enough," I growled.

She widened her eyes. "B-but ..."

"Enough," I growled again, grabbing her hand.

If she wanted to constantly demean herself, I would force her to tell me what she loved about herself. I would force her to rip away all her insecurities and just be present with me. Happy. At fucking peace with herself.

I didn't care how long it'd take. I didn't care what happened between us.

All I wanted was for her to love herself and to see how intelligent she really was.

CHAPTER
THIRTY-TWO

HEATHER

HECTOR SAT in a maroon-cushioned chair in the corner of the room at Radiant, leaning back and watching me carefully. His eyes were even darker than usual under the dim light, his stubble peppered with gray. "Take off your shirt for me."

As if there were people watching us, I looked around the room. We were alone in one of the private glass rooms, but nerves still pricked at my stomach. Hector had seen me naked countless times, but now, he was asking me to strip for him!

How was this going to make me feel better about myself? He had been mumbling something like that since we'd snuck out of the office together without Dad noticing. And yet every time I'd asked him, he'd just kept on saying that I'd see.

But I wasn't seeing anything!

"Take. Off. Your. Shirt."

After swallowing hard, I unbuttoned the first button on my shirt. Then the next. And the next. "Wouldn't you rather take my clothes off for me?" I asked because I felt anything but sexy, fumbling with the buttons.

"No."

Once I popped off the last button, the shirt slipped down my shoulders. It dropped at my feet, leaving me standing in my skirt, shoes, and lacy bra.

I reached around my body to unclip my bra next, but Hector said, "No."

"You don't want me to strip for you?" I asked.

"Hand me the shirt."

I picked up the shirt from the ground and gave it to him, but before I could release my hand, he wrapped his hand around mine.

"Now," he said, voice quieter and softer than it usually was, "tell me what you love about yourself."

My eyes widened. "What?"

"Tell me what you love about yourself."

I opened and closed my mouth a handful of times, nothing coming out. What did I love about myself? Why was he asking me this now—when I felt the least bit sexy, stripping for him in a completely silent room?!

"Heather," he said, "now."

The first word that came to my mouth was *nothing*, but I kept my lips sealed.

"I ..." I started, heart pounding. "I like the way I look after I shower in the morning."

He released my hand and laid the shirt on his lap. "Next piece."

Is he going to make me do this with every piece of clothing?!

Once I tugged off the next piece of clothing, I handed it to him and stayed quiet, desperately trying to rake my brain for something that I liked about myself, something that I was proud of, or something that made me smile.

But ... I came up with nothing.

"Heather," Hector warned, his hand wrapping around mine once more, "tell me."

"I like ..." I started, trailing off. "I like how I can be myself around my friends."

He held my hand tightly for another moment, as if he wasn't going to accept that as an answer, and then he finally released my hand and nodded for me to continue. I unclipped one of my heels and stepped out of it.

He extended his hand, as if waiting for me to give him a single shoe.

"Do I have to compliment myself for each shoe?" I whispered.

"Yes."

I pressed my lips together and handed him the shoe. Tears welled up in my eyes as his fingers touched mine, and I opened my mouth, but no words came out because I had nothing left to say about myself.

"I love that you're hardworking," Hector said for me, taking the shoe.

My lips quivered as I reached for my left heel. I handed it to him.

He set the pair of shoes on the ground near his feet. "I love how bold you are."

Tears trembled in my eyes. I stared at him, expecting him to follow up with, *But your brother is so much more hardworking than you, But your brother has done so many more bold things than you have* … but the words never came out of his mouth.

"Please continue," he said softly.

With trembling fingers, I shimmied out of my skirt and handed it to him.

"I love your drive to be successful."

"Why aren't you saying anything about my body?" I whispered, hating that his words were bringing tears to my eyes and making me feel things that I never had before.

If he complimented the way I looked, I wouldn't feel so … emotional right now.

My looks were the only thing I had that my brother didn't.

"Because you're worth more than just your beauty."

Tears stung my eyes. "Please don't make me take off any more."

He held out his hand. "Take off your pantyhose for me."

Throat closing up, I peeled off my pantyhose and folded them in my hands, not wanting to give them to him because I didn't want to listen to another compliment. All I had wanted when I signed up for this was to learn how to be a submissive. I hadn't expected all these emotions.

"Hand them to me," he said.

"No."

"Why not?"

"Because I'm scared," I whispered.

He held out his hand. "Give them to me, Heather."

After staring at him for a couple of moments, I whimpered softly, holding back a sob, and handed him the pantyhose. I stared at the ground, feeling so bare—and not just because I was almost naked in front of him.

Terror ran through my body. *What is he going to say this time?*

Once he took them from me, he gently lifted my chin and made me look him directly in the eyes. His gaze was soft and, dare I say, safer than I had ever seen it. He smiled and drew his thumb across my chin.

"You're fucking vibrant, Heather. Approachable. Respectful. Eager." He pulled me into his lap and wrapped his arms around my waist to pull me close, his lips hovering over mine and his warm breath fanning my face. "You're sympathetic and tender, fond and curious."

My lips quivered, and I almost burst out into tears before he placed his lips on mine.

"And best of all, you're mine."

CHAPTER
THIRTY-THREE

HEATHER

"CAN you pass me that knife, hon?" Hector said from the other side of the island.

Hon?

My eyes widened slightly as I reached for the knife in the knife block. Water boiled on the stove, and the scent of freshly made pasta sauce drifted through my nostrils.

I grabbed a utensil and handed it to him. "Here you go."

Where did hon come from? He has never called me that before.

Our fingers skimmed against each other as he took the knife from me. He turned to the sausages to cut them for the pasta with a small smile written across his face, the same warm smile that ached to tug onto my lips.

I turned back to the stove, stirred the pot of penne with a huge wooden spoon, and watched the water bubble. Even after our scene had ended, I still had all the feels about what had happened, how Hector forced me to tell him everything I loved about myself, which wasn't much. At times, I hadn't known what to say, and he'd had to fill in.

Warmth spread through my chest. I felt like he could've

stripped hundreds more clothes off me, and he still wouldn't have run out of things that he could say—things that I didn't believe myself, but he did. I rolled my shoulders forward. He really did.

"What're you thinking about?" Hector said, looking over from the sausage cut.

"Nothing."

"Heather."

"Hector," I said in an amused tone.

Once he set down the knife, he walked over to me and trapped me between him and the counter. I hummed softly and leaned back to look up into his pretty, safe eyes. Who would've thought that I'd be making dinner with Hector Patton after he took me to his BDSM club?

Definitely not me.

"Don't make me ask you again."

"My thoughts are private."

"Not when I can read them all over your face." He wrapped his hands around my thighs, picked me up, and set me on the counter. Then, he stepped between my legs, running his hands up my thighs. "I know that look."

"What look?" I asked with a smile, playing dumb.

"*That* look."

Not really wanting to get into it right now, I grabbed my spoon. "Taste this pasta."

After picking up some penne on the spoon, I lifted it to his mouth. He wrapped his lips around it and tugged it into his mouth, chewing while his playful gaze was on me. Butterflies fluttered through my chest.

"Did you mean what you said back at Radiant?" I asked in a whisper.

Of course my dumbass had to ask while he was in the middle of chewing.

Once he finished, he placed his hands on the counter beside me. "Yes."

"Really?"

"Yes." He paused. "Why?"

I chewed on the inside of my cheek and stared into his soft eyes, wondering *how* anyone could be so nice to me and really mean it. All the time, my parents compared me to my younger brother, and I always lived in the shadow of his accomplishments.

My lips quivered, and hot tears built in my eyes. "Because … I've never felt special."

From the outside, I was sure that it looked different. My parents spoiled me and always gave me everything that I wanted. They paid for my apartment with Sierra and had let us stay at the cabin by the beach this past fall for a vacation.

I didn't have a hard life compared to most people. I was privileged.

While I pressed my lips together to steady them, I couldn't hold back a stray tear from falling down my cheek. I wrapped my arms around his shoulders and pulled him toward me, resting my head on his shoulder.

Yet … all they talked about in front of me was my brother. All they bragged about to their friends when I went out with them was my brother. All they seemed to care about was how successful he was and how unsuccessful I had been, especially with failing software development last semester.

I might've had it all, but I didn't feel special. To anyone.

He captured me in his arms and drew me closer, holding me tighter than anyone had ever held me. I gripped on to him, clutching his shirt in my fists, like if I didn't, then he would disappear into thin air.

Bubbles burst in the pot beside us, nearly boiling over … but I couldn't care less.

"I've never felt special to anyone," I whispered after a sob, "except to you."

THIRTY-FOUR

HECTOR

AFTER I DREW my fingers through her hair to soothe her, her words continued to replay through my mind. I was the only person in her life that made her feel special, and I didn't want to admit it, but she was that person for me too.

In the past five decades of my life, I hadn't felt special to any of my family or my subs.

Except her.

The aroma of spices drifted through my nose from our half-finished dinner. Water bubbled over the edge of a pot on the stove, steam pouring out. I held Heather tighter, not ever wanting to release her.

My heart thumped quickly in my chest. "I feel the same with you."

She placed her chin on the center of my chest and looked up at me, eyes filled with tears. "You don't have to say it back, Hector. I just ... I wanted to let you know how much I appreciate you. I'm not good with this kind of thing."

"I mean it," I whispered. "I can't believe how lucky I am to have you."

In the kitchen, bathed in warm light, Heather smiled up at me, her lips quivering slightly. Her pretty eyes sparkled when the moonlight gleamed on them the right way, and I had never … ever felt the warmth in my chest with anyone else.

Everything about us was wrong.

But I wasn't going to stop. I wasn't going to give this up.

Not now … maybe not ever.

After pushing away some tears, she smiled up at me.

And yet, while she made me feel safe, anxiety nipped at my insides. Since our little affair had started, I had always feared that she'd leave me, but now, what I feared most wasn't that she'd leave me … but that I'd lose her.

If Jacob ever found out about my relationship with his daughter, it would shatter our friendship and unravel the life and the business that I had built with him for the past half a decade of my life. What would my life be without business? It was what I'd dedicated every waking moment of my life to before her.

Hands curling around her waist, I pulled her toward me and placed my mouth on hers. She arched her back and pushed herself against me, her fingers curling around my collar. I moved my lips against hers, desperate to taste more of her.

I had kissed her so many times now, but I couldn't help myself.

She had made me hungry to taste her, hungry to be with her.

How can I wait any longer to be more than just a Dom to her?

After tugging off her shirt from her shoulders, I dropped it to the ground and left her standing half naked in my kitchen without a bra. I fondled her breast and ground her into the counter, my cock throbbing inside my pants.

"I need you," I mumbled against her lips. "Now."

She wrapped her arms around my shoulders and spread her legs. I ran my hands up her thighs and gripped her ass, and then I kissed down her neck, sucking on the skin. She moaned softly as the water bubbled in the pot.

At this rate, we'd just have to order something because dinner wasn't being made.

But I didn't care.

Just as I sank my hand between her legs, someone knocked at the door. I moved my fingers against her clit, biting and sucking on her skin hard enough to leave a bright red hickey. The knock came again.

"*Fuck*," I growled.

When I tried to ignore it for a third time, the bang became louder.

"Finish up here," I said, stepping around the kitchen island. "It's probably a delivery."

Not sure why anyone would be delivering anything this late at night, but I wasn't normally home during the day. If it was something important—like a certain something that I'd ordered for Heather the other night—then I didn't want it sitting out in the hallway.

Before opening the door, I glanced over my shoulder at Heather, humming to herself and stirring around our dinner in the stainless steel pot in nothing but a pair of pants. My lips curled into a small smile, and I pulled the door open.

My eyes widened as I stared at Heather's father.

What the fuck is he doing here?

"Hector," Jacob said. "Sorry about popping in so late."

"Jacob," I said, loud enough for Heather to hear so she'd hide, "what's up?"

The very last person that I'd expected here was Heather's father, especially this late at night. If Heather tried to hide in the bedroom, she'd have to cross the room, and Jacob would see her, so I hoped to God that she had ducked behind the counter.

Instead of staying in the hallway, Jacob walked into my apartment. "We need to talk."

CHAPTER
THIRTY-FIVE

HECTOR

WITH A TIGHT CHEST, I swallowed hard and shut the door gently behind him, stiffened in fear that he had seen her or that he already knew that we were together. Maybe he had seen us at Radiant. Maybe Evelyn had said something to him about us.

My heart thumped wildly against my chest when I turned around to see him heading to the fridge, something he hadn't done since we'd started our business years ago when he came over for a beer to talk through start-up problems.

Water bubbled in the pot on the stove, and, my God—

Heather's purse was on the counter, and some of her clothes were scattered across the floor.

Fuck!

When Jacob turned to grab a beer, I grabbed Heather's purse from the counter and placed it on the island chair in front of me so he wouldn't see it. After cracking open the bottle, he turned around and leaned on the opposite side of the counter.

Heather crawled around the corner just in time so he didn't see her and stopped a few feet from me, half naked and her eyes as wide as saucers. My throat was dry, but I swallowed again, heart pounding.

"I have to talk to you," Jacob said.

"Can we do this tomorrow?" I asked, desperate to get him out of here. "It's late—"

"I'm sleeping with Evelyn."

And I'm sleeping with your daughter. Now, leave.

Heather's clothes were still littered around the room, and I didn't know how Jacob hadn't seen them yet. I ran a hand through my hair as Heather crawled closer to me until she sat at my feet, staring up at me through those eyes.

I peered down at her, tightening my jaw at how fucking sexy she looked, teasing me.

"I know that you are," I said to Jacob.

Heather moved closer to me and placed her mouth on my bulge. I tensed and sucked in a sharp breath, tangling my fingers in her hair to pull her closer. God, I was going to fucking hell for this, but I didn't care.

"You do?" Jacob asked, looking up. "How?"

"Come on," I said. "My family owns Radiant."

"You've seen us together?" he asked.

Heather moved her mouth up and down my bulge, then undid my zipper. I tilted my hips forward just slightly as my cock sprang out of my pants and smacked her in the face. Almost immediately, that brat sucked my head into her mouth.

"Yes," I said, biting back a grunt.

After swirling her tongue around the head of my dick, she sucked me all the way into her throat until her lips met my groin. I looked down and clenched my jaw, seeing those eyes stare up at me.

She is just begging to be punished, isn't she?

While she had her hands around my thighs, I gently pushed them off. She locked them behind her back, her tits bouncing as she moved back and forth on my dick. I swallowed and looked up at her father.

"And?" Jacob asked, like he expected more of a response from me.

"Don't let HR catch you."

I usually would *never* respond like that, but Heather was behind the counter, sucking my cock and basically begging me to fuck her right here, right now, while her father was still in the room. And, God, it took *everything* in me to keep control.

"Are you being serious?" Jacob asked.

After taking a stronger hold on Heather's hair, I moved her back against the kitchen island so she couldn't pull her head back. I stepped closer, forcing my cock down her throat and pinching her nose closed.

I would come deep down her throat if I heard her gag.

God, the thought is so fucking hot.

Her gagging over and over on my cock while her father stood across from me, wondering what the fuck was going on. It was so wrong, but I couldn't stop, especially when she tried to pull her head back. I kept her in place and very discreetly pushed my dick deeper.

My balls were heavy, slapping against her chin with every thrust.

"Yes," I grunted. "What they don't know doesn't hurt them, right?"

Jacob took a sip of his beer. "Right."

Heather's tits pressed against my thighs, her nipples hard. When I peered down briefly, I saw she had pushed a hand between her legs to rub her aching little cunt.

Fuck, what a horny little bratty girl I have on my hands …

"Well, okay then …" Jacob said.

But he couldn't leave now.

Because if he did, then he would see his daughter sucking my cock behind the island.

"You'd better make sure that the others won't blab to HR either," I said, thrusting my dick.

"Others?"

"The other executives who are also fucking her."

Jacob stiffened. "How long have you known?"

"A while."

When I finally pulled all the way out so she could breathe even though I wanted her choking on my cock in front of her dad, she sucked in a small breath. I looked down at her to see her eyes filled with tears, her mouth wide open, and her tongue out.

Ready for more.

I grabbed her chin and thrust my dick back down her throat, hitting the back of it hard. I dropped my hand to her throat and wrapped it around the front to feel my dick nestled inside it, massaging myself.

She moved even closer to me and sealed her lips around the base of my cock, cutting off the little air she had left to breathe and tipping me over the edge. My hips seized, and I held her head tightly on my dick so she would be forced to swallow every last drop.

While I didn't see myself ever leaving Heather at this point, she wasn't ready for her father knowing about us, so I held back a grunt. And truthfully, neither was I. We would be in a bad place, business-wise. We had to be more careful.

Yet … that was becoming increasingly harder around Heather.

CHAPTER
THIRTY-SIX

HEATHER

THURSDAY AFTERNOON, I sat in Carnegie Coffee Company, listening to the soft hum of laughter and clinking of cups from other customers. I leaned back on the couch, sipped on my hot chocolate, and stared out the foggy window at the snow drifting down from the gray sky.

While Sierra, Athena, and Sun gathered next to me at the corner table, all I could seem to think about since last night was Hector. My friends made me so happy, yet nobody had ever made me feel the way that he did.

"So, spill the beans!" Sierra said. "What happened with Hector and your professor?"

A smile tugged at the corners of my lips as I glanced around at my three best friends, all of them eager for a juicy story to come from my mouth. And, boy, did I have the juice today, especially after yesterday.

"Oh, nothing much," I hummed, purposefully dragging it out to make Sierra plead.

"Come on!" Sierra exclaimed, sipping her hot chocolate.

"You have to have something," Athena said. "You wouldn't be

so cheery today."

Unable to hold it back any longer, I leaned forward. "Hector literally made him pee his pants!" I giggled, remembering the way that Eric had stumbled out of the office yesterday with pee covering his suit pants.

"Oh my God!" Sierra giggled. "He. Did. Not!"

"Did too."

The girls broke into a fit of laughter.

"That's not even the best part."

"It gets better than that?!" Athena asked, clutching her belly.

"Hector literally made Eric crawl on his knees to me and beg for forgiveness."

While I had been so nervous to be in control, the memory of it felt oh-so good. To see the professor who had antagonized me for two semesters, begging to be forgiven for what he had done and me having the power *not* to forgive him …

I shivered.

Man, that did something to me.

Sun giggled softly behind her hand.

"Please tell me that's not all," Athena said. "This is golden. I need more."

"Well …" I chewed on the inside of my cheek, feeling like my life was a reality TV show. "After that, I got really insecure. We ended back up at his place to make dinner together, and my dad walked in on us."

"What?!" they all exclaimed at the same time.

After I shushed them, I leaned over the table. "Don't worry. He didn't see anything. I had to crawl around the kitchen island so he wouldn't see me. And I ended up giving Hector head while—"

Sierra wiggled her brows. "Those Patton boys love getting their dick sucked."

My lips curled into a small smirk.

"Wait." Athena paused. "You sucked him off while your dad was in the same room?"

I bit back a smile and nodded.

Sun broke out into a fit of uncontrollable giggles. While she usually was quiet, I knew that she loved every bit of gossip from our friend group. We would have to bring her to Radiant one of these days. She'd get a kick out of it.

"Damn, do they have any more brothers in this family?!" Athena asked.

Sun nudged her. "You have Charlie."

Athena rolled her eyes. "Oh, please. He would never do something like that! He's too sweet, and besides, for the millionth time, we're just friends! Nothing would ever happen between us like that."

"Mmhmm," Sierra hummed.

After leaning on my hand, I looked outside and smiled, still lost in my own little world and still thinking about the way that Hector had made me feel all last night. "He makes me feel so special and happy."

Sneaking around in front of my father—literally feet from him... damn! I still can't believe I did that!

"Stop," Sierra said, hand on her chest. "It's making my chest all warm and fuzzy."

My cheeks flushed, and I kicked my legs back and forth underneath the table. "He's my dad's best friend, but I think I love Hector," I whispered more so to myself, but it came out louder than I'd expected.

While my friends were excited, a moment later, their expressions dropped.

"Heather?" someone asked behind me.

My eyes widened, and the happiness drained from my body.

Oh my God!

"Heather," Mom said behind me again.

With nerves shooting through me, I turned my head to see her holding her cup of coffee so tightly that some spilled over the edge and drizzled down the blue cup. Her lips were parted slightly, the look of shock written across her face.

"You're seeing Hector?"

HEATHER

AFTER SUCKING in the thick aroma of hot chocolate and disappointment, I stared at Mom through wide eyes. My mouth was hanging open, and I couldn't get myself to close it ... because Mom had just learned my deepest secret.

"Mom," I whispered, standing.

Sierra scooted out of the way, the girls quiet. I shuffled in front of the table toward Mom, who mirrored my surprise. She gripped her iced coffee so tightly that the cap had popped off and beige-colored liquid now ran down her hand.

Another silent moment passed, and Mom gulped. "Heather, sweetheart, we need to talk."

When I grabbed my belongings from my seat, the girls sent me sympathetic looks.

Mom clutched her purse tighter and offered Sierra, Athena, and Sun a tight smile. "Don't forget about the holiday party this weekend, girls." She cleared her throat. "You're all invited, along with your plus-one."

With that, Mom twirled around and headed straight out the doors. I followed after her through the snow mixed with rain and toward her car. She slipped into the driver's seat, and I debated whether I should just run home at this point.

Heart pounding inside my chest, I slipped into the car and shut the door.

An awkward silence filled the car.

"Heather, is it true?" Mom asked. "Are you really involved with your father's best friend?"

My cheeks flushed red with embarrassment. I looked down at my thighs, unable to meet Mom's gaze. "Yes," I admitted, my voice barely audible. I placed my hands on my bouncing legs. "We're in a relationship."

"He's your father's best friend," she whispered. "Twice your age."

"I'm sorry." Tears filled my eyes. "I didn't mean for it to happen. It just did."

"How does this just—" Instead of finishing her sentence, Mom paused and sucked in a sharp breath. "Listen, Heather ... I understand that emotions can be complicated, but you need to realize the consequences of your actions. This is going to hurt your father deeply."

"He's not going to find out," I said. "Promise me that you won't tell him."

"Heather," she said, voice even softer, "he will find out."

"Give me some time to figure things out," I pleaded. "Please."

Mom pressed her lips together. "Fine, but in the meantime, I'm going to talk to Hector."

"Mom!" I exclaimed. "You can't. Please."

If Dad heard even a bit of this, he was smart enough to put it all together ... and if he found out, then I would become an even bigger disappointment in his eyes. And just recently, Hector had ... made me feel like I was enough.

I didn't want that all to be ruined.

"There needs to be some ground rules laid out," she said.

"I'm an adult, and there were rules. You read them over."

She tilted her head to the side slightly. "Hector is older than me, Heather."

"So, why does that matter? Dad's dating someone my age."

As soon as the words left my mouth, I smacked my lips together because I wasn't supposed to know about that, and if I wasn't supposed to know about that, then Mom definitely wasn't supposed to know.

They had been divorced for a couple of years now—all on good terms—but it still felt weird.

"Your father is dating someone your age?" she repeated, brows raised.

"I'm not supposed to know," I whispered. "Please don't tell him that either."

After taking a couple of deep breaths, she looked straight ahead through the windshield. "I won't tell your father any of this, but I need to talk to Hector. I'm not going to let him take advantage of you." Her voice softened, and she peered over at me. "You're still my little girl."

"Hector isn't taking advantage of me," I said, a small smile on my face. "Anything but ..."

She reached over the center console and tucked a strand of hair behind my ear. "Baby ..."

"He makes me really happy, Mom." My heart fluttered at the thought of yesterday, at what he had done *for me*, how he'd made me feel. "He makes me feel like nobody else ever has, like I'm important and special."

"Have your father and I made you feel any less than that?" she asked.

I pursed my lips together and dropped my gaze. "Sometimes, Dad does."

"I know he's hard on you and your brother, but he loves you. You know that, right?"

"It doesn't feel like it," I mumbled.

Mom pulled me into a hug. "I'm sorry it doesn't feel that way. Want me to talk to him?"

"No!"

"Not about you and Hector, but about—"

"No," I said. "It's fine."

After a couple of moments, Mom nodded. "Okay. I won't tell your father, but after work tomorrow, I'm going to talk to Hector."

"Mom!" I exclaimed. "Why? I just explained everything to you."

"Because," she said with a smile, "if you're dating someone, then I'm going to make sure they have the best intentions with your heart, sweetie. Nobody hurts my girl, or we'll sue them straight into the ground."

"I don't think that's how it works." I giggled, a weight lifted off my shoulders.

She smirked. "If he breaks your heart, I can make it work."

While I didn't think Hector would do that—maybe I was too optimistic after last night—I leaned my head against Mom's shoulder and stared at the sleet pounding down on the windshield. "Thanks, Mom."

THIRTY-EIGHT

HECTOR

JACOB and I sat across from each other in a conference room, along with Evelyn and a few other executives, poring over charts, numbers, and figures in our annual review of the health of our business.

I ran a hand over my face, unable to focus because I couldn't stop thinking about last night. When Jacob had walked into my place and Heather crawled around the island to suck on my cock … *fuuuuuuck, I loved it.*

"So, we need to …" Jacob started.

But I completely zoned out when I lifted my gaze and saw Heather's mother walking into the office from the elevators. Dressed in a gray suit jacket and a briefcase slung over her shoulder, she headed straight for our conference room.

What is she doing here?

When she made eye contact with me through the glass wall, I cursed under my breath. A moment later, she knocked on the door and opened it like she owned the place.

Jacob stopped short and glanced over quizzically. "What are you doing here?"

Evelyn sat up taller and looked between them, jealousy on her face.

But I knew that Heather's mother wasn't here for Evelyn. She was here for me.

"I need to talk to Hector," she said firmly, her eyes locked on to me.

I shifted in my seat, not wanting Jacob to think that anything was going on between me and his ex-wife. What a goddamn mess that would be. I straightened out the cuffs on my suit and sucked in my cheek. This feeling of uneasiness around a woman's parents was unfamiliar.

"This isn't the best time," Jacob said, glancing at the documents spread across the table.

"It's important, Jacob," she said, not backing down. "Please, just a moment with Hector."

After Jacob shot me a puzzled look, as if to ask what this was all about, I nodded and stood because I really didn't need any questions right now. Especially not in front of everyone. Jacob stepped to the side, gesturing for me to leave.

I followed Heather's mom out into the hallway and made sure to shut the door tightly behind me. While the meeting continued without me, I could feel Jacob's gaze on us the entire time I stood there.

"If you break her heart, I will break yours," she snapped. "You understand me, Patton?"

"Heather told you?" I whispered.

"No." She crossed her arms. "I overheard her talking with her friends."

Sighing softly to myself, I ran a hand over my face, trying to find the right words to explain myself. She probably thought that I was taking advantage of her daughter, using her for some sick reason.

"Do you realize the gravity of this? You're dating your business partner's daughter!"

"I know," I said, taking her elbow and leading her farther

away from the conference room so Jacob didn't overhear anything that neither of us wanted him to know. "It's complicated. I never intended for things to turn out this way, but … I …"

She crossed her arms. "You what?"

I dropped my gaze to the ground and smiled softly. "I love her."

While I could tell she had just been about to give me hell for dating her daughter, she paused and stared at me with an unreadable expression on her face. Then, she nodded.

"I have no intentions of hurting her," I said honestly. "She is the sweetest woman I know."

"She is," she said with a curt nod. "So, don't hurt her, whether it's your intention or not."

"I won't. We have a contract."

"I know. I read it over."

Another long pause.

"Of course," I said. "So, you know she can leave whenever she wants."

My chest tightened when the words tumbled out of my mouth because it hurt, just thinking about Heather leaving me at this point. I fucking loved her, and I wanted to make her the happiest she could ever be. I didn't want to see any more of those tears.

"I've accepted it, but … Jacob won't," she said. "So, he must not find out. Not yet."

I let out a relieved breath. "Heather and I will figure out how to handle things properly."

She nodded and looked through the glass wall. "Is that the girl that Jacob is dating?"

My eyes widened. "What?"

She rolled her eyes. "Oh, come on. I know that you know what I mean."

"If you're speaking about Evelyn and Jacob, then …" I sucked in a sharp breath, not wanting to give away all of Jacob's secrets, but also not wanting Heather's mother to out us. I didn't think Heather—or I—was ready for that. "Yes."

After looking into the glass wall to the conference room at her ex, she nodded and walked off. I stared at her retreating figure, wondering what would happen next. For as long as I had known her, she always kept a level head. She was a lawyer after all.

But what did this mean for her daughter and me?

A couple of moments later, the door behind me swung open, and Jacob cleared his throat. "Everything all right out here?"

I nodded.

"What was that all about?" he asked.

I walked back into the conference room. "Nothing for you to worry about."

And, God, please don't ask about it either.

CHAPTER
THIRTY-NINE

HEATHER

SATURDAY NIGHT, the Christmas party was in full swing at Mom's house. Fire crackled in the living room fireplace while warm lights cast a festive ambience throughout the entire house. I sipped on my wine at the piano with my friends.

"So, how'd your mom take it the other day?" Athena asked, sitting on the seat in front of the piano.

Charlie sat beside her, dressed in a suit that matched Athena's dress. They said that they hadn't planned to match, but Charlie definitely did.

"Well, she hasn't told my dad yet." I glanced over at Dad and Hector chatting. "I hope."

"Did she actually go visit Hector at work?" Sun asked.

"Yes."

Sun's cheeks reddened in embarrassment *for* me. "Jeez."

"Yeah, I think my dad now thinks they're sleeping together."

"Ew," Athena said, then followed up with, "Your mom's hot and all, but her and Hector?"

"Please don't put the image in my head," I hummed. "He's mine."

Charlie chuckled. "Possessive already over him?"

I cut my gaze to him because I could say a whole shit ton about him having been suspiciously possessive over Athena lately. He smacked his lips together—as he should—and turned around toward the piano, playing keys out of tune.

"Sorry that we're late!" Sierra said from the front door.

Finally, she's here!

"Sierra," Mom said, eyeing Hector's brother, Steven, "you brought a boyfriend."

Sierra stiffened and glanced up at Steven. "He's just a friend."

Oh my God! What is wrong with her? Why would she say he's just a friend?!

Mom smirked at their hands. "Seems to be a little more than just friends, but never mind that." She turned to Steven and furrowed her brow, looking him up and down. "I know you from somewhere, don't I?"

"I'm Hector Patton's brother," Steven said.

"Hector and my ex-husband are business partners and the best of friends," she said, peering over her shoulder at me and giving me those *what the hell is happening, why didn't you tell me about this* eyes. "That must be it."

After Mom grabbed the bottle of wine from Sierra, she ushered them into the house and toward the living room. I shot up from the piano and headed toward her, stopping short when Hector got their first. I didn't want Dad thinking anything was going on outside the office.

"Didn't think you'd be here," Hector said to Steven.

"This is Sierra," Steven said, introducing my best friend to Hector. "Sierra, this is Hector."

"We've met before," Sierra said. "I've seen him at some of Heather's mom's parties."

"Ah, yes," Hector said.

"And I'm Heather's friend."

Hector paused and glanced past her to me. I avoided eye

contact with him and wiggled my brows at Sierra, happy that she'd finally found the courage to ask Steven on a date.

"I'm gonna say hi to my friends," Sierra said, looking at us.

As Sierra headed over, my gaze lingered on Hector, who smirked softly at me, giving me those eyes that said that he'd have his way with me before the night was over. Hector loved sneaking around.

"Does your dad know?" Sierra asked. "About you and Hector?"

"Of course not!" I exclaimed. "Do you think I'm a masochist?!"

"Maybe." Athena chuckled from the couch. "You're crazy."

"I am not," I hummed.

"So, Sierra, since you're sleeping with his brother, is Heather right? All the Patton genes are good ones?" Athena winked and sipped on her champagne.

"Athena, they're both adopted," I said.

She playfully rolled her eyes. "You know what I mean."

"Don't think she does," Charlie said, lips curled into a smile. "Why don't you explain it?"

Athena shot Charlie a playfully dirty look, then shoved a dessert into his mouth. "Shut it."

"What?" Charlie said, mouth full of cookie. "I didn't say anything wrong."

"You're trying to embarrass me," Athena said.

Charlie finished chewing. "You're trying to embarrass Sierra."

"Yeah, but she's cute when she's all flustered."

Charlie smirked. "So are you."

An hour into the party, Sierra disappeared somewhere with Steven—probably to hook up. I sat on the couch with Sun, talking about how I wanted to bring her to Radiant at some point because we all knew she was secretly a freak.

"No," Sun said, hiding behind her hands. "I'd be so embarrassed."

"It's not that bad. What are you into?"

Sun's face reddened. "Heather!"

"Are you bullying poor Sun over here?" Mom asked, walking over with champagne.

"No …"

"Yes, she is," Sun said.

After tsking, Mom sat on the couch beside us. "So … Sierra just disappeared onto the balcony with Hector's brother. Are they …"

A giggle left my mouth because she loved the drama, didn't she?

"Yes, they're dating," I said.

Mom shook her head. "What am I going to do with you girls?"

I followed Mom's gaze to the balcony that they had supposedly disappeared onto and smirked. "Maybe you should give Sierra a stern talking-to. I'm sure she would love that and wouldn't be em—"

After arching her brow, she brought her drink to her lips. "She'd be *so* embarrassed."

My lips curled into a small smile, and I caught sight of Hector chatting with Dad at the other side of the room, yet his gaze hadn't left mine since I'd greeted him when he arrived earlier. Butterflies fluttered in my belly.

Hector tapped Dad on the shoulder and excused himself, gesturing for me to follow him right before he slipped into the hallway that led to the guesthouse. I cleared my throat and jumped up, not even caring anymore if Mom knew.

She'd keep her mouth closed.

"Well, I'll talk to you later, Mom."

And with that, I discreetly followed Hector into the back hallway. A door opened down the hallway, and Hector slipped into it. I followed. Once inside, the door closed softly behind us, and we were finally alone.

CHAPTER
FORTY

HEATHER

HECTOR PRESSED me against the door, peppering kisses up and down the column of my throat, the faintest tinge of alcohol on his breath. With his body flush against mine from behind, he ground his huge bulge against my ass.

I pressed my fingers into the door and moaned softly. "Hector, don't stop."

"I can't stop thinking about what you did when your father came to my place the other night," he murmured into my ear, shoving two of his fingers between my pussy lips and onto my clit. "I have been so hard for you all day."

Another whimper left my mouth, and suddenly, he turned me around so my back was pressed against the door. Then, this man dropped to his knees, put my legs on his shoulders, and lifted me so his mouth was between my legs and I was in the air.

Eyes rolling back, I gripped a fistful of his hair and yanked him closer to me, unable to hold back my moans. He moved his fingers in quick circles around my clit.

Except it wasn't half-assed, like how most guys ate pussy. Hector was hungry.

So, I decided to play with him.

I tugged harder on his hair. *"Good boy."*

He pulled away and smacked my clit hard. "You know better."

After a moment, he returned to eating my pussy, his dark and angry gaze on me. My lips curled into a smirk, and I let my legs rest easily on his shoulders as I pulled him even closer to me.

"Be a good boy and eat."

Really, I just didn't think I would be able to last much longer.

Hector pulled himself away from me, dropped me back on the ground facing away from him, and yanked off his tie. After wrapping it around my mouth like a gag, he tightened it and bent me at the hips.

Instead of thrusting his cock deep into my pussy, he slapped my clit. "I try to reward you, and you have to be a brat." Another slap, and there was nothing soft about it. It was hard and stung, made to hurt.

"You should've kept—" I began, words muffled.

"You should keep that pretty little mouth shut," he growled, slapping my pussy again. "It's not like anything coherent can come out of it now anyway with all that spit rolling down your chin." He rubbed it in, ruining my lipstick. "Think about your next words carefully, brat."

"Your punishments are—"

Before I could finish my muffled sentence, footsteps shuffled down the hallway. I smacked my lips closed, in case it was Dad, and stared up at Hector. He captured my pussy lips between his forefinger and his thumb, squeezing it slightly, then slapping my swollen clit with his other hand.

I yelped and then placed a hand over my mouth to muffle the sound.

"Stop pressuring her so much," Mom said to someone in the hall. "She's your daughter."

"I haven't pressured her to do anything," Dad responded.

Inside the room, Hector slapped my clit even harder. I banged my head against the door and bit my lip to hold back a groan. My clit was so sensitive now, and all I wanted was for him to plunge his huge cock deep into my pussy.

"Heather is going to work under me once she finishes school," Dad said.

"Did she tell you that's what she wanted?" Mom argued.

Hector smacked my clit again, his mouth on my ear. "You're mine," he hissed. "Say it."

I pressed my lips together, fearful that I'd moan if I opened my mouth.

"Jacob, you stress her out too much," Mom said.

God, she had that right.

"Say it," Hector growled into my ear again. "Or else I'll make you scream it."

"How do I stress her out?" he asked. "It's work. Everyone's stressed out."

"Not you, apparently," she said. "Especially with your secretary."

My eyes widened at their conversation just feet from us, but Hector did not give a fuck as his hand came down repeatedly on my clit. I grasped on to his shoulders, digging my nails into his muscle, and bit back a scream.

"I'm yours!" I cried. "I'm yours. I'm all yours."

FORTY-ONE

HEATHER

SITTING on Mom's white bubble sofa with a blanket wrapped around my shoulders, I sipped on my hot chocolate and rested my head on Hector's shoulder. Fire crackled to my right, the gentle pattering of snow outside drifting through my ears.

Hector sighed beside me, the fire glowing in his eyes.

I closed my eyes, enjoying the moment. Everyone else had left the party about an hour ago—even Dad and Evelyn—but I lingered with Hector because … it was nice to be able to be around my family, not having to hide.

The fire warmed my face. After I exchanged a few soft glances with Hector, he set his hot chocolate on the coffee table and took my hand. Snow continued to fall outside the window, creating a blanket of white on Mom's front lawn.

"I want to talk to you about something."

Nerves fizzed in my stomach. "What is it?"

"What are your plans after you graduate?"

After taking a small sip of my drink, I swallowed. "Is this about me being your full-time submissive?"

"No, this is about your future."

My lips curled into a frown. "I don't know. Find a job at a company, doing business?"

"I thought you didn't like business school."

"I do, but …" I sighed. "You heard my dad tonight at the party. My brother is off building his own company, and Dad is trying to force me into yours. I think he thinks that I don't have a plan for after I graduate, and he's right. I don't know what I want to do."

"That's okay."

"No, it's not," I said. "I have one more semester left of graduate school. I'm twenty-four."

"I didn't have my life figured out at twenty-four," he said.

"Yeah, but that's different."

"How?" Hector pushed. "Steven was off building his own company right out of high school. He went to college, was offered funding by all these investors, but he turned it down, and he sold his company a couple of years ago for over a billion dollars."

I twisted on the couch and stared at him.

"Heather …" He pushed some hair out of my face. "You can do anything. At any time."

After sighing because it was easier to not have my life together than to do something I loved and fail at it, I rested my forehead on Hector's shoulder. "I think it'd be cool to have my own company, but the idea of starting from scratch intimidates me."

"What about it intimidates you?"

"I'd be responsible for my own success and my own failures."

"And?"

"And what if I found no success at all?"

"Then, you'd still be doing something that you love. Then, you would've tried when most people don't try at all." He paused. "What if you do succeed, Heather? What if you do something that you love for the rest of your life? How would you feel then?"

A nervous laugh bubbled up from my stomach.

"Huh?"

"I'd be happy." My smile faltered. "But do you think I can actually do it?"

"Your dreams are worth pursuing, no matter what anyone else thinks. Only you can make them come true and only you will care about them as much as you do. Other people won't care about your goals, nor will they put forth as much effort to achieve them."

"Once we're finally open with our relationship," I whispered —that was, if we ever ended up being open and not a secret in front of Dad—"then I want you to be proud of me. I don't want to be a disappointment."

"The only way you'll disappoint me is if you don't try. Your happiness depends on you."

"But that's so scary," I murmured.

"Well, it's good that I'll be there to support you through it all. Huh?"

A mixture of emotions welled within me—fear, hope, and determination. But above all else was the gratitude that I had for Hector. Even though my insecurities continued to plague me ... he stayed by my side and supported me, no matter what. He made me feel like I could conquer any challenge that lay ahead of us—both in my professional and in our personal life.

The fire crackled and cast dancing shadows across the room.

"It's getting late."

After setting my hot chocolate on the coffee table, I stood and headed over to the front entrance to grab our coats from the closet. Mom lingered by the doorway, sipping on a coffee, even this late.

My cheeks warmed at the thought of her watching me with a man twice my age, but she hadn't said much more to me since our original talk a couple of nights ago. Butterflies fluttered in my stomach. She, at least, hadn't told Dad yet.

"You look so happy," she whispered. "I haven't seen a smile that big in a long time."

"Mom," I said, even more embarrassed, "not in front of him."

"Oh, he can't hear me over the fire." She waved my comment off. "When you told me about your relationship with Hector, I was nervous that he had all the wrong intentions with you. But I've known him for a long time, and I have never seen him so at peace than I have tonight. He's tender with you."

My lips curled into a smile, more butterflies fluttering around inside me.

"I love him," I whispered.

"You should tell him."

"But what if he doesn't say it back?"

She laughed. "Oh, Heather, I don't think you have anything to worry about."

CHAPTER
FORTY-TWO

MOM LIVED about twenty minutes outside the city, so our ride home was longer than usual. But I didn't mind the silence that engulfed the car as I watched the snow drift down on the highway around us.

"I love the holidays," I whispered. "It's so pretty during this time."

We pulled off an exit that led to downtown Pittsburgh. The soft glow of city lights shimmered through the falling snow. Every year, the city came alive with festive decorations that adorned every corner and lights that shimmered in the square.

I chewed on the inside of my cheek, wondering if I should invite him to Christmas dinner with my family. The thought of it made my stomach turn because I didn't think I'd be able to resist sending him flirty glances, which Dad would definitely see.

"So, what are you doing for Christmas?" I asked.

"Usually, I host Christmas at my place and cook for Michelle and Steven. But Steven has asked to host Christmas at his high-rise this year, so I'll be celebrating over there." He paused for a moment, his hand tightening on the steering wheel when we pulled to a light. "Do you want to come?"

"I, um …" I paused and bit back a smile. "Only if you want me there."

He reached across the center console, wrapped his hand around the front of my neck, and pulled me closer. "Your pretty ass had better be there," he murmured against my lips. "I'm not spending Christmas without my good girl."

"Good girl?" I hummed. "I don't know about that."

He arched a brow. "You're not my good girl?"

"Nope," I said, popping the *P*. "But I'll come to dinner as your brat."

"You know," he hummed, pressing on the gas when the light turned green, "I was beginning to think that you've earned yourself a collar, but if you're going to be a bad girl and call yourself my brat, then—"

"Just kidding!" I exclaimed. "I'm your good girl!"

A chuckle escaped his mouth. Instead of heading back to his high-rise, Hector took another exit and started up the mountainside. Pittsburgh was a sea of hills, but this one led up to Mount Washington, which overlooked the city.

"I don't think so," he said.

"I am!"

"Prove it."

"Prove it?" My lips curled into a small smile, and I reached over the center console to grasp him through his pants. I stroked him up and down through his suit pants, growing warmer every moment. "Does this prove it to you?"

After grunting and groaning softly, he turned into a parking lot at the top of the mountainside and parked the car. Before I knew it, he had swept me over the center and into his lap, and then he opened the door. He walked with me in his arms out of the car and set me in front of a black steel railing.

Hector wrapped his arms around me from behind and pulled me closer, burying his nose into the crook of my neck. The crisp winter air chilled my skin, and my breath caught in my throat at the breathtaking view of the entire city of Pittsburgh adorned in twinkling lights beneath a blanket of falling snow.

From behind, he trailed his hand up the back of my thigh and up underneath my skirt to grip my ass. He pulled back on my hair with his free hand. "You're my good girl, so say it," he murmured against my neck. "Tell everyone you're my good girl."

My lips curled into a smirk. "No."

With his body pressed against my side and his huge bulge grinding up against my ass, he spanked me hard. I yelped, a wave of heat coursing through my body to my pussy. Instead of asking me again, like he usually did, his hand came down on my ass again.

"Hector!" I whimpered.

Still no chance for me to tell him I was his good girl.

Another smack. This time harder.

"H-H-Hector!" I sputtered, pleasure coursing through my body. "Please."

Every time he smacked me, his hand inched lower and lower, until he had officially bent me over the metal steel bars of the city overlook and spanked my cunt.

"I'm your good girl!" I cried, needing it. "I'm your good girl!"

After pulling back my hair with his free hand again, he wrapped his other hand around the front of my neck and placed his mouth on my ear. "Good girl. You're actually learning for me. And for that, you'll get a reward when you get home."

"A reward?!" I asked, eyes growing wide.

"Only good girls get rewarded," he murmured. "As long as you're good on our ride back."

I smiled softly as Hector pulled my skirt back down and pressed the wrinkles out of it, gently rubbing my ass. Heat coursed through me, and while I couldn't wait to get back now … I wanted to savor this moment with him on top of Mount Washington.

"I don't want to hide our relationship forever," I whispered, curling my fingers around the black railing. "But I also don't want to cause any problems between you and my dad, especially business-wise."

"It doesn't matter what happens between your father and me."

"Yes, it does," I murmured, breath caught in my throat. "Because I love you."

My words hung in the air, and for a moment, time stood still. The snow continued to fall gently around us. I sucked in a breath in anticipation, heart pounding inside my chest and thoughts whizzing through my head.

What if he didn't say it back? What if it was too soon? What if I ruined this—

Within a moment, he twirled me around and cupped my face in his big hands, a smile painted on his lips. "God, I love you too, Heather." And then he leaned in and kissed me hard on the mouth.

FORTY-THREE

HECTOR

THE LOW BUZZ OF CHATTER, mixed with the clacking of keyboards, drifted through the air. I stepped out of the elevator and loosened my tie, ready for the day to be over so I could leave with Heather, who hadn't stopped teasing me since she had come in at lunch.

Jacob leaned against his office doorframe, arms crossed over his chest and gaze on me. It wasn't the soft, lighthearted one he usually gave everyone, but a sterner one that I had rarely seen before.

"Hector," Jacob called from his office door, nodding me over to him.

I sighed internally and briefly glanced in Heather's direction. She stiffened and widened her eyes at me, as if to say, *Please don't let this be what I think it is.* After a moment, I pulled my gaze away and continued my strides toward Jacob.

"Is something wrong?" I asked.

"Let's talk."

Before I could say another word, Jacob walked into his office and left the door wide open. I sucked in a deep breath, preparing myself for whatever it was that he wanted to talk about, and then I stepped into the room.

When I closed the door behind me, Jacob let out a sigh. "How was the party?"

"It was great, as usual," I said. "Leann sure knows how to throw a Christmas party."

"She does," he said flatly, taking a long drag of his coffee. He strummed his fingers lightly on his desk and cocked his head. "You stayed a bit longer than the others, didn't you? Anything happen?"

Fuck.

"Not much."

"Nothing?"

After clearing my throat, I stuffed my hands into my pockets. "You know how it is, Jacob. Leann loves to chat." *If I keep running my mouth like this, then he'll probably think that I'm fucking his ex-wife —if he doesn't already.*

"Must have been quite the evening for you to stick around that long."

Fuck.

While I meant to laugh lightheartedly and to brush it off, my chuckle came out strained. "Yeah, well, she's a great host. And you know," I hummed, trying desperately to find a way to get out of this, "I'm not one to rush off."

Damn, I can't stop lying. Jacob knows I hate staying late.

"Sometimes, people stay later for reasons other than good conversation, don't they?"

I peered through the windows of Jacob's office and outside into the main office. Except she wasn't working. I could tell by the strained look she was giving me and the tenseness of her shoulders.

"What are you insinuating?" I asked Jacob, meeting his gaze.

"I'm not a fool, Hector, so don't treat me like one," Jacob said.

My heart beat faster inside my chest, my fingers tugging at my collar. Part of me thought that maybe I should tell him about me and his daughter now to get it over with. But if he was this tense at the thought of me fucking his *ex*-wife ... I couldn't imagine what would happen when I told him the truth.

"I don't take you as a fool." I straightened my back to show him that he couldn't intimidate me. "But I'd like to know what you're trying to accuse me of before responding because whatever you think I'm doing, I'm not."

Every day, my relationship with Heather was becoming a more and more dangerous game that could cost us both everything. But it was a game that I wasn't going to quit; it was one that I had become addicted to.

Jacob tightened his jaw. "You're sleeping with my ex-wife."

I blew out a sigh of relief. "No, I'm not."

He didn't pull his gaze away. "First, she came into our office during our quarterly meeting to talk to *you*. Next, she got very flirty during the Christmas party. Then, you decided to stay after I left. What time did you even get home on Saturday night?"

"She was not flirting with me during the Christmas party. She was being friendly."

"I've never seen her be that friendly with you," he said.

"I don't know what to tell you. I'm not sleeping with her."

"You'd better not be lying to me, Hector, because secrets have a way of slithering out."

My gaze became distant again, focusing on Heather heading to her desk outside the office windows. *She* was my deepest secret, but I really didn't know how long it would be before that secret slithered out. Her confession in my car on Saturday night had set a fire within me.

The memory of snow drifting down around us, her leaning closer and whispering that she loved me. *Me!* A man twice her age, whose best friend was her own father, and whose worst fear was losing her.

"I'm not lying to you," I said. "But why does who I date matter to you? In case you've forgotten, you came to my house the other night, half drunk off your ass, stressed out about being involved with Evelyn."

Jacob stiffened. "Evelyn is a different matter. This is my ex-wife."

"So? Do you still have feelings for her?"

"No, of course not." Jacob grabbed his coffee mug. "But if you started dating her, then our business partnership would become messy. And we have something really good. This company is growing faster than any other ones I've run."

Well, if he only knew ...

"I'm not dating your ex-wife" —*I'm dating your daughter*—"so you don't have to worry."

HEATHER

"HEATHER," Dad beckoned from his office. "Come here. I'd like to talk to you."

My mouth dried, and I pushed back my swivel chair from the makeshift desk that Dad had set up for me to *learn the ropes* of this business. I peered through his office windows at Hector, who sat slouched in a chair across from Dad's desk, rubbing his forehead.

Oh my God. If he knows …

After shuffling some papers and stacking them neatly on my desk to buy myself some time, I smoothed out my skirt and headed toward his open door. Evelyn shot me a pitiful look, and I wanted to make a break for the elevators, but I forced myself to continue walking.

"How's it going today, sweetheart?" Dad asked when I walked into the room.

I shot Hector a glance, but he barely looked in my direction.

Damn it, this seems worse than I thought!

Even if we waited a hundred years, I didn't think that I would be ready for this conversation. How could I tell Dad that I was dating his best friend and business partner, who was twice my age and into BDSM?!

"It's going good," I whispered, almost unable to breathe. "Why?"

"Just wondering," he hummed. "I had a conversation with your mother on Saturday."

Did Mom rat me out?! She was so cool with it!

"Oh?" I asked. "About what?"

"She told me that I was being too hard on you."

Hector cleared his throat. "I should get back to work."

"No. No, it's fine," Dad said. "This concerns you too."

My stomach tightened into knots. *Fuck.*

"I'll be quick with this," Dad reassured Hector, and then he turned back to me. "Your mother told me that you might not want to work here and that I might be making you feel like you have to work here with us. If I—"

"It's fine," I mumbled. "I'm used to it."

"Heather," Hector said suddenly, now looking in my direction. "If you don't want to work here, you don't have to." He looked as if he wanted to say more, to expand on our conversation on Saturday night, but Dad could never know about that, so he pressed his lips together. "Okay?"

"Mmhmm," I hummed, knowing that a direct *yes* was what he was looking for.

An *mmhmm* might get me in some good trouble later.

I headed back to the door. "I'm going to go now."

No polite asking my father—or Hector—if I could leave. In the corner of my vision, I watched Hector's fingers twitch on the chair, probably aching to spank me. My lips curled into a small smirk, and I turned all the way around to show him that he could do *nothing* here.

"Wait," Dad said.

I rolled my eyes and then twisted my head to face him. "Yes?"

Dad pulled out a chair next to Hector and across from his. "Hector, you can go now."

"I don't mind staying," Hector said, watching me trudge all the way to the chair and sit beside him, his dark gaze never leaving mine once. "We have a couple of things to talk about anyway once Heather leaves."

After taking a seat opposite of Dad, I played with the end of my skirt underneath the desk.

Hector discreetly reached over and laid his hand on my thigh, digging his fingers into my knee, as if to say, *Watch yourself, brat.*

"So …" I hummed, paying no attention to Hector.

"Your mother also mentioned a boyfriend."

Double fuck!

Hector stiffened in the seat beside me, his fingers not moving anymore against my knee. I shifted uncomfortably in my seat and looked anywhere besides at Dad because I didn't want him to get any more ideas than the ones he already had.

"Why haven't you told me about him?" Dad asked.

Maybe because you'd freak the fuck out!

"I've just been really busy with school and work," I lied.

Dad leaned back in his chair, lips curling into a small smile. "Tell me more about him."

My knee bounced, and I chewed on the inside of my cheek. "Oh, um … he's this really nice kid that I go to school with."

As soon as the words left my mouth, Hector gripped my thigh harder. "Some kid at your school, huh?"

"Yep."

He drew his hand up my thigh, getting dangerously close to my pussy, and hummed.

"When are you going to bring him around?" Dad asked. "I want to meet him."

Oh boy, Dad … you already have.

I pushed Hector's hand off me and stood up. "We're just casual right now."

Hector tightened his jaw, his gaze snapping to me and darkening. I walked to the door, knowing that he could do nothing but simmer in his jealousy and possessiveness, and pulled it open, a smirk drawn across my lips.

I was sure that I'd be seeing him later.

HEATHER

"BY THE END OF TONIGHT, you're going to wish you had kept your mouth shut."

Hector sat in the driver's seat next to me, his hand gripping the steering wheel and his teeth gritted. He hadn't said a word to me since he had picked me up from my apartment, and now ... he was threatening me with a good time.

"I doubt it," I hummed.

After clicking his tongue, he pulled into his reserved parking spot in the parking garage underneath Radiant. The bright overhead light illuminated his white knuckles, and I couldn't stop myself from giggling. All this just because I'd said he was a casual fling.

Which we *both* knew wasn't true.

"Are you seriously angry over this afternoon?" I asked, rolling my eyes for added effect.

Once he shut off the car, he blew out a long breath and turned his head toward me, his fury disappeared and replaced with ... contentment. I furrowed my brows, hating that he was suddenly okay now. I mean, wasn't he just pissed?!

"No." He smiled. "I'm not."

I flared my nostrils because this was *not* how it was supposed to work. "But—"

He exited the car. "Come with me."

"No." I crossed my arms and stared at him through my window. "What's wrong?"

"Nothing's wrong, Heather. Follow me."

Because he wasn't giving me the reaction that I so desperately wanted, I narrowed my eyes and refused to move from my spot. I wanted him angry, possessive, and jealous over my words this morning. So much so that he drilled that punishment into me nice and hard.

"I'm not coming."

A moment passed, and Hector nodded. "Fine."

When he turned away and began walking to the entrance of Radiant, I leaped out of the car and ran after him. "Fine?! That's all you have to say! I literally told my dad that we were just casual and that you were just some boy, and you—"

Before we could make it to the entrance, he had me pressed up against the building, his hard cock on my stomach and his breath on my ear. "We both know that you're just trying to be a brat. So, drop the little act before I make you cry tonight."

Warmth gathered between my thighs. "You won't."

"Mmm," he murmured, moving his lips closer to mine. His warm breath fanned my lips, and he was millimeters away from crashing his lips onto mine and kissing me with everything he had. "Is that so?"

"Yep."

His lips curled into a devilish smirk, and he took my hand and led me into the club. My breath hitched, a shiver of anticipation rushing through my body. His grip on me was tight; his annoyance at my disobedience was back.

"I don't think you're going to have any harsh punishment for me," I hummed. "It's going to be the same old, same old with you tying me up and trying to make me beg for you. And I always just give in because I feel so, so bad for you."

As soon as we stepped foot into Radiant, Hector released my hand. Instead of heading straight up to his private glass room, he walked to the bar area, where people could chat and watch others get themselves off.

I followed after him quickly because I didn't want to be left alone here and slipped between him and a barstool.

He leaned across the bar to order us two drinks, then looked down at me. "You hate my punishments that much, yet you follow me around like a puppy dog."

"I do not."

"You know what your punishment is going to be tonight, *brat*?" he asked, unbuttoning my shirt in the middle of the bar. I grasped his hands to get him to stop, but he continued popping off the buttons, leaving me in my bra and skirt. "Why don't you take a guess?"

"Hector," I whispered, cheeks warming as people started to look over at us.

"What? The brat can't take it?" he hummed, reaching behind me to unzip my skirt.

It fell to my ankles, and I held my hand over my thong. "I-I can!"

The bartender slid two glasses across the counter, and I went to grab one. I needed to down something if Hector was going to make me walk around, practically naked, at a goddamn sex club!

"This isn't for you." Before I sipped the drink, Hector grabbed it from me. "Follow me." He started walking away and smirked back at me. "Or you can continue to be a brat and stand there, half naked. Choice is yours, Heather."

When he was halfway across the bar, I followed after him to a couple on a black leather couch. The woman was sitting on, what looked to be, her husband's lap, smiling at Hector, then looking back at me trailing behind him.

"Is this your submissive?" she asked.

"Yes, this is Heather," Hector said. "Heather, this is Russ and Maya."

"Hi," I squeaked, suddenly so self-conscious.

Hector handed Russ one of the glasses, then took a sip of his own. "Heather has decided that she wants to be a brat for me tonight, so she's come over here to ask you what her punishment should be."

My mouth dropped open, and I shook my head. "I ... we ..."

Russ took a sip. "Did she break any rules?"

Hector leaned against the armrest and looked at me, awaiting a response. "Did you?"

I opened and closed my mouth a handful of times, growing embarrassed and insecure. "Yes," I whispered.

"Which rule?"

"Following his directions."

"His?" Maya asked. "Who's his?"

"I mean ..." My mouth was dry, and I looked to Hector for guidance, but he didn't say anything. *Oh my God, I hated this!* I rubbed my sweaty palms together. "I ... didn't follow Master's directions."

"And it seems she doesn't know—or willingly refuses to use—honorifics," Russ noted.

My cheeks burned hotter, and I peered at Hector. "Wh-what should my punishment be?"

"You're not asking me," Hector said. "You're asking Russ. Look at him when you speak."

I looked at Russ, my entire body feeling like it was on fire, and I swallowed hard. "Wh-what should my punishment be for disobeying Master?" I whispered, the words so foreign and awkward on my tongue.

Maya giggled softly. "It depends on how much you're willing to make amends." She leaned closer to me and smiled. "How much do you want to please your Master, Heather?"

FORTY-SIX

HEATHER

"I WOULD DO anything to please him," I whispered, nerves shooting up and down my arms.

Hector relaxed on the couch beside Russ, his dark gaze on me and one brow lifted. "If you would do anything to please me, then you wouldn't have been a brat, now would you? Are you lying to them, Heather?"

I sucked in a sharp breath, nipples taut, and shook my head. "No, Sir."

Maya shifted in Russ's lap, their curious gazes on mine. He moved his hand up and down his wife's thigh, getting higher and higher every single time. I swallowed hard, wondering if Hector would do that to me in front of everyone, and pressed my thighs together.

"Maya says that you should be humiliated," Russ said.

My eyes widened, and I looked from Russ to Maya and then to Hector.

"Humiliated?" I whispered. "H-how?"

Hector curled his lips into a smirk, chuckled, and stood up, his hand coming around the front of my throat and tipping it back, so

I stared back and up at him. "I think I have a couple of ideas. And if you're good, then I'll go easy on you."

"If I'm bad?" I whispered, excitement rushing through me.

Russ chuckled from the couch. "Brats never learn."

Hector didn't peel his gaze away from me once, his smirk stretching further across his face. "See, the thing about brats like you, Heather … I love taming them. It might take weeks, months, even years, but you will learn."

My lips curled into a small smile, the others around us seeming to fade away when I was with him. I didn't mind that I was half naked in the middle of his sex club. All that mattered was that his attention was on me, and mine was on him.

He released his grip on my throat and trailed his fingers down my body, unhooking my bra from behind. I sucked in a sharp breath and pressed my thighs together, heat exploding through my body.

The straps of my bra slipped down my shoulders, and Hector tore it off my body so I was bare to everyone around us. Then, he shoved me down to my knees in the middle of the bar and seized my chin.

"You're going to show everyone how terrible you are at giving head."

"Terrible?" I repeated, brows furrowing and anger rushing through me. "I'm not terrible!"

Another low chuckle escaped his mouth, and he unbuckled his belt with one hand. I glared up at him, feeling as if I had something to prove in front of a bunch of experienced men and women because he wasn't about to make me look like I had no clue what I was doing.

I might've been a virgin when I met him, but that didn't mean I didn't know how to make him come down my throat. So, as soon as his belt came off, I grabbed at his pants to help him the rest of the way.

He wrapped his belt around my throat, buckling it at its tightest setting and yanking up on it. I pulled out his huge cock and sucked the head into my mouth almost instantly, swirling my tongue around it and flicking the bottom, just how he liked it.

He traced a featherlight path across my jawline, his gaze dark. "Look at this little whore, desperate to show her Master how skilled she is, to prove herself to him." He tangled his hand into my hair. "This is how you should act every night."

After swirling my tongue around his head once more, I sank my mouth down onto his cock and stuffed as much of him as I could into my throat until my lips met his groin. And even then, I stuck out my tongue and flicked it against his balls.

Hector grunted softly, thrusting his hips back and forth, his cock hitting the back of my throat. He pulled back on my head until his cock fell out of my mouth and smacked against his thigh. I crawled toward him, desperate to prove myself, to show everyone that I wasn't bad at this.

And just when I took him back into my mouth, someone gasped to my right. "Heather?"

With Hector's cock still buried in my throat, I looked over at the bar and spotted Dad.

FORTY-SEVEN

HEATHER

AFTER GRABBING a blanket to hide my body from Dad, I quickly stepped behind Hector. My heart pounded inside my chest.

This couldn't be happening right now. This couldn't be happening right now. This really couldn't be happening right now!

"Heather?" Dad repeated.

But instead of disbelief and shock, this time, his voice was filled with a thunderous anger.

Cheeks burning, I shuffled further behind Hector, unsure about what to do. I didn't want to cause a scene in Hector's club, but Dad had pretty much already caught everyone's attention with his booming voice.

"What the fuck are you doing here, Heather?!" Dad exclaimed.

"Dad, I …" I whispered, struggling to come up with some explanation.

He stepped toward us. "Are you fucking seri—"

Hector placed a hand on Dad's chest. "Don't talk to her like that."

My eyes widened, and I flickered my gaze up to Hector, who shoved Dad away so he couldn't get any closer. Fuming in anger, Dad furrowed his brows and finally shifted his gaze away from me and to Hector.

"You're supposed to be my best fucking friend," Dad spat, his words dripping with venom. "My business partner that I trust. And you go on, fucking my daughter in a fucking sex club?! How long has this been going on?"

"Dad," I whispered.

Dad pointed a finger at me. "I'll scold *you* lat—"

Hector seized Dad's finger and broke it right in half, the crack echoing through the bar, the music so dull compared to Dad's scream. Hector grabbed Dad by the jacket and dragged him out into the hallway. "I told you not to talk to her that way."

As soon as they were out of earshot, I ran around the bar like a madwoman, looking for my clothes, which I couldn't seem to find anywhere. Michelle, Hector's sister, appeared beside me, ushering me into another room and handing me some spare clothes.

"Why don't you wait here for a bit?" she offered.

But I was already out the door and running through the hallway toward a back door, where a couple of security guards were standing around, which meant that Hector and Dad had to be out there, right?

Once I pushed through them, I slammed open the door and spotted Dad and Hector glaring at each other in the alleyway. Hector held his gaze steady, his jaw clenched, as if he were preparing for Dad to hit him.

Dad clenched his fists. "How fucking dare you betray my trust like this!"

"This isn't about you," Hector growled, seemingly not having noticed me yet. "I love her."

Dad flared his nostrils. "She's my daughter! You've been a part of our lives for years, Hector. And I trusted you. This is how you repay me? By sneaking around with my daughter? Using her to get off? Telling me that nothing was going on?"

"Dad, please, just listen," I pleaded from the door, tears welling up in my eyes. "It's not like that. He's not using me. I … we …" I started, losing my voice somehow halfway through my sentence. "I love him too."

"He's twice your fucking age, Heather."

"Yeah, and you're twice Evelyn's age!" I exclaimed, walking down the steps. "Why does it even matter?! He's not using me, and Mom accepts us. Why can't you ever just be happy for me?!" I hiccuped. "You never can."

Releasing his clenched fists, Dad cradled his finger and pursed his lips together. Instead of saying another word, he turned on his heel and stormed down the alleyway to the street, then turned a corner and disappeared.

I flared my nostrils and ran after him. "Where are you going?! I'm not done!"

This wasn't fair. He didn't get to just leave. He didn't get to just be disappointed in me anymore. Just because I was his daughter didn't mean that he could disrespect me or push me into a career that I didn't want. Sure, Mom had talked some sense into him. But she shouldn't have had to do anything.

Why couldn't he have accepted me from the beginning, like he had with my brother? Why was his disappointment constantly aimed at me?

And I knew, deep down, that I would never hear the fucking end of this.

When I made it to the street, Hector grabbed my elbow. "Let him go."

"No!" I shouted. "This isn't …" Tears burned my eyes, and I suddenly felt the weight of the world crushing my shoulders. "This isn't fair." I buried my face into his chest and gripped on to his shirt. "This isn't fair! He's so hypocritical."

Hector wrapped his arms around my shoulders and pulled me closer to him, my heart thumping heavily inside my chest. I rested my forehead against him and cried so loudly because I didn't care to keep us a secret anymore.

It was over.

The secret was out.

Dad was disappointed.

Wind whistled around us, and I gripped on to him even tighter. "What if … he never forgives me?"

As much as I wanted to say *screw him*, as much as I wanted to say that I didn't need his approval, I so, so, so, so, so, so desperately wanted it. I wanted Dad to be proud of me. I wanted him to love me, to accept me. He was my father, my blood.

"There is nothing he needs to forgive you for," Hector said. "You've done nothing wrong."

"I slept with you," I whispered. "I love you."

Hector scooped my chin into his hand and forced me to look up at him. "Is that wrong?"

I swallowed hard, realizing what I had just insinuated, and shook my head. "No, but—"

"But you're an adult. I'm an adult. We both can make our own decisions about who we love and who we want to be with. There was nothing non-consensual that happened between us, so he has nothing to forgive you for, okay?"

After wiping my tears with my sleeve, I nodded. "Okay. I just never wanted to hurt him."

Hector pressed a gentle kiss to the top of my head, his lips a whisper against my hair. "I know, and he'll understand that too. But I promise you that no matter what happens, I'll be by your side. You're not going to face him alone. You'll never face *anything* alone."

CHAPTER
FORTY-EIGHT

HECTOR

FROM THE KITCHEN, I watched Heather bundle herself up in blankets and plop down onto the couch, tears still heavy in her eyes from tonight. While this was a problem that we would both have to face, I didn't quite care about the consequences of Jacob finding out about me and his daughter. At least not as much as Heather cared.

After turning the stove up to high, I slipped a pan onto it.

What pissed me off the most was the way he had talked down to her.

She had always told me that Jacob was hard on her, but I had never seen it. I had believed that he might put her under pressure, but it wasn't until I'd heard the tone of his voice tonight that it really hit me.

I tossed some food onto the pan and drenched it in olive oil, my mind racing. I had snapped that man's finger without a second thought about the consequences to protect her, and, God, I would do it again.

Heather sat on the couch, bundled in three blankets and whimpering softly to herself. Moonlight flooded into the room from the large windows, shining off Heather's silky hair. The doorbell buzzed, and Heather raced to it.

When she pulled open the door, Heather's mother and Sierra rushed into the room. Steven, who was dating Sierra, waltzed in after them and shut the door quietly behind himself, peering over his shoulder to look at me.

"Did you talk to him?" Heather asked her mother.

"No, sweetheart, but please calm down."

Heather burst out into tears. "He's so disappointed in me!"

Heather's mom hugged her. "Your father loves you, and he'll come around eventually."

"No, he won't!" Heather cried.

Sierra gently rubbed her shoulder.

While I wanted to console her, Steven found his way to the kitchen. He wasn't much of a cook, but he grabbed the spatula from me and shooed me out from behind the stove.

"So much for you being a good cook." He chuckled. "You're burning this."

I ran a hand through my hair and sighed heavily. "It's been a bit of a night."

He cracked half a smile that didn't make it to his eyes. "Sierra filled me in."

After placing my hands on the counter, I leaned back onto it and stared up at the ceiling. "I don't care that he knows, but she does, and it's fucking tearing me up on the inside. I hate seeing her cry."

"How'd he find out?" Steven asked.

"We were at Radiant," I said softly.

"*Fuck.*"

"Yeah, fuck," I murmured. "Before I left work, he told me that he was spending the night with his assistant at her place, and then this fucker walked right into our club. It's my fault. I should've been more careful."

Steven let out a breath. "He walked in on you together. *Damn.*"

"In the middle of a punishment," I said, crossing my arms. "I don't think that he'll hurt Heather, but I'm worried what he'll say to her and what this will mean for our business. I let my emotions get the best of me and broke his finger."

Steven glanced up from the food. "I'm sorry. You broke his finger?"

I ran a hand over my face again. "Long story."

"I can tell. You keep jumping around all over the goddamn place." He paused and moved the spatula around in the pan, not knowing what the hell he was doing. "You think he might try to sabotage your business?"

"I don't know," I said honestly. "He has connections, and he's not one to shy away from using them if he's pushed too far. I have seen it many, many times while we were climbing to the top. Now, I'm the one who's pushed him."

Steven leaned against the opposite countertop. "So, what's the plan?"

My gaze flickered up to meet Steven's. "Hell if I know."

I glanced back into the living room and sighed softly, watching Heather's bottom lip tremble. All I knew was that I didn't quite care as much about what happened to the company as long as I could protect Heather.

CHAPTER
FORTY-NINE

HEATHER

SOFT CITY LIGHTS flooded through the large windows in Hector's high-rise. I lay in his bed, my chest heavy with guilt and my mind racing with images of what Dad had walked in on earlier. Hector's entire dick had been in my mouth.

I squeezed my eyes closed, trying to erase the memory. Distant sounds of traffic and the occasional city murmurs drifted through my ears. Hector tightened his grip on my waist, his warmth spreading through my body.

And yet I still couldn't sleep.

Minutes stretched into hours, and the darkness in the city only became light.

The confrontation with Dad replayed in my mind, his anger and disappointment cutting deeper than any blade could. I hadn't been ready to tell him. I hadn't prepared myself yet. I wanted to make him proud of me first at work, and this had done the complete opposite.

Hector's steady breaths against my ear played like a soothing rhythm. Even with everything going on, even though I'd acted crazy by crying all night just because I wanted my father to not be disappointed in me, Hector stayed by my side.

He traced patterns on my arm, and I let my gaze look into the distance, to the city skyline beyond the windows. Pittsburgh was twinkling with Christmas lights, yet I didn't feel the holiday joy. Would Dad ever find it in his heart to forgive me? Could I ever make him proud?

After gently squeezing me, Hector pulled me closer. "Can't sleep?"

I turned my head to meet his gaze, the moonlight casting a silvery glow upon his handsome face. I sank down in the bed and allowed my lips to quiver once more. They had barely stopped since earlier.

"No," I whispered. "I can't stop thinking about my father."

Hector brushed away a stray strand of hair that clung to my tear-streaked cheek. "I know it's hard, Heather. But you need sleep."

In the distance, light glimmered through the city skyscrapers, pinks and golds painting the sky. I gripped my phone on the opposite side of my body and tilted it up to see if Dad had returned any of my messages.

Me: I'm sorry.

Me: I didn't mean for you to find out this way.

Me: Can we please talk?

I had texted him in hopes that he'd respond, but it had been hours with nothing.

My eyes welled up with tears, a weight on my chest almost suffocating me. I squeezed the phone even tighter in my grip and forced it down by my side. Hector shifted beside me to face me and reached for my phone.

"Heather," he murmured, "you can't keep torturing yourself like this."

"I just ... I need to hear from him."

Gaze softening, he pulled the phone out of my grasp and set it on his nightstand. Then, he lay back down and cupped my cheek with his hand. "I know how much this means to you, but give him time to process this. Sending him texts won't help."

My lips quivered. "He'll never be proud of me. How did this even happen?"

Hector swiped away a tear that had escaped down my cheek with his thumb, his touch gentle. "We made choices, Heather. And now, we have to face the consequences. But that doesn't mean he isn't proud of you."

"Oh, come on," I said. "He has never been proud of me. And he never will now."

"Is he not proud of you, or are you not proud of you?" he asked.

"Stop," I whispered, wrapping my arms around myself. "I …"

I didn't like how he always called me out on my bullshit. He didn't have to force me to face … how I truly felt. How I didn't feel good enough because I had followed my brother's footsteps in order to please Dad.

Light continued to seep into the room, and my eyes became heavy. I sank back into the pillows and closed my eyes, still upset but so exhausted over everything that had happened in the past twenty-four hours.

Once Hector adjusted the blankets around me, he rose from the bed. "Get some rest, Heather. We'll talk about … *this* tomorrow." He crossed the room and drew the curtains closed so it was dark.

While I didn't want him to leave the bed without me, I really needed the sleep. My phone buzzed on the nightstand, and I snapped my gaze to it. Hector scooped up my phone and walked toward the door.

"Hector, wait," I said. "Is that him?"

"I know you're hurting, Heather, but constantly checking for his messages won't make things better," he whispered, tilting the screen upward and peering at it. "But if it'll help you sleep, it's not him."

"Will you wake me if he responds?"

"No."

"But—"

Hector walked to me and placed a kiss on my forehead. "Sleep, hon. You need it."

CHAPTER
FIFTY

HECTOR

WHEN I STEPPED into the office, a current of hushed conversations and curious glances charged the atmosphere. I sucked in a low breath and continued to my office, ignoring the stares because it wasn't any of my business.

Well, it was my business. But I didn't care what they thought.

Heather needed me to be strong, and I didn't have remorse for falling in love with her.

After Heather had slept through the morning, I'd cooked her breakfast and made sure she was all set with everything that she needed for today. She wasn't going into classes, and I didn't blame her.

I dumped my bag off at my desk and walked back into the main workspace, spotting Evelyn. She sat at her desk with papers in front of her, but her gaze was on me. When she noticed me staring back, she stood.

Once she made it to me, her face scrunched into a mix of concern and uncertainty. "Hector, can I talk to you for a moment?"

"Of course. What's going on?"

Evelyn sighed, her gaze troubled as she met my eyes. "Jacob

has been in his office since this morning, with the door locked and the curtains drawn. I've never seen him like this, Hector. He's devastated about what happened."

Guilt ate away at my heart because while I wasn't remorseful about my relationship with Heather, I still respected him ... just not the way he had been treating her at the club, pointing fingers and raising his voice.

"I didn't expect him to be at Radiant last night. He told me that he would be with you."

Evelyn's expression softened. "We were planning on staying at my place for a bit, but ... it's kinda messy on my end right now." She looked around and chewed on the inside of her cheek. "If I had known you were there with Heather, I wouldn't have suggested Radiant."

"It's okay."

She frowned. "Is there anything I can do? Should I try talking to him again?"

I blew out a long breath. "You don't have to get in the middle of this. If he wants to lock himself in his office"—*like a baby and not have a real conversation with me*—"then let him stay there. He's pissed—and rightfully so."

After a curt nod and a sympathetic smile, she returned to her desk. I grabbed some coffee from the break room and checked my phone to see if Heather had messaged me yet. I didn't want her crying all day at my place.

A calendar event reminder popped up on my phone, and I groaned.

Meeting in two minutes. Second floor.

Once I stirred some sugar into the coffee to keep me the hell awake, I grabbed a notebook from my office and headed to the elevators. Just as I stepped into the hallway, I jogged to an elevator that was closing and slipped my arm between the doors.

The elevator doors slid back open, and I stepped inside, only to freeze when I spotted Jacob standing in the corner, dark bags underneath his eyes. When he saw me, he tightened his jaw and glared ahead.

Fuck.

The doors closed, leaving us alone, and the silence stretched on and on between us. The air was charged with unsaid words and heavy tension. I cleared my throat, needing to get this out for Heather's sake.

"Jacob, we need to talk."

Jacob snarled, "I don't know what there is left to say, Hector."

I bit my tongue before I said something out of line. "Look, I understand you're angry, and you have every right to be after what you walked in on last night. But Heather has been texting you all night, wanting to talk."

Jacob's eyes blazed with intensity. "Don't pretend you care about my daughter."

"I do," I said honestly.

"If you truly cared, you wouldn't have let this happen behind my back!"

"I do care about her, more than you might want to believe," I said, hand tightening into a fist. "But you're not the only one hurting here. Heather is hurting, too, and she needs both of us to act like adults and find a way forward."

"Move forward? You fucking broke my finger last night over this!" he shouted, holding up his hand to show me the finger bandaged. "You were face-fucking my daughter! You think this can just be brushed aside?"

"I broke your finger because *you* were pointing it at Heather like she deserved it," I said through gritted teeth. "I don't think that this should be brushed aside, and I'm not going to beg for your forgiveness for loving your daughter when you haven't."

"When I haven't?!" Jacob exclaimed, the doors now wide open on the second floor.

When neither of us left the elevator, the doors shut again.

"You're asking me to accept what you've done?"

My lip twitched. "I'm asking you to put aside your anger and consider what's best for Heather. She's torn. She's been crying all night. She's gotten less than three hours of sleep because she's worried that you'll never be proud of her."

Jacob flared his nostrils. "You have no right to tell me how to handle this."

"Then, start acting like a man and not a stubborn child who's throwing a tantrum!"

I wanted to hold it all in, but Heather was being more of a damn adult than he had been. He could've texted her back, told her that they'd talk later, that it was late, that she should get some sleep.

"Get your head out of your ass and talk to your daughter. Tell her you love her," I growled, hitting the Open Door button. "If you're going to blame anyone, blame me. Not her. She deserves to feel loved by you. Not hated."

CHAPTER
FIFTY-ONE

HEATHER

THE AROMA of freshly brewed coffee enveloped our cozy corner of Carnegie Coffee Company. I kicked my legs back and forth underneath the table and stared at my computer screen that had gone dark.

Fingerprints smudged the screen, but I hadn't found the energy in the past two years to clean it off. Sierra, Athena, and Sun sat beside me, cracking jokes in a much-appreciated attempt to get me to smile.

I leaned toward Sun and rested my head on her shoulder, frowning. Dad hadn't texted me all day, but Hector had mentioned that he had spoken with him while they were at work. He didn't give me any more details than that.

Which meant that the conversation probably hadn't been good.

"I just can't believe it," I whispered. "He literally walked in on us."

Sun rested her head on mine and gently patted my hair. "It's going to be okay."

"Yeah, he'll get over it," Sierra said. "Don't worry about it."

"But—"

"Girl, he is dating someone our age. He doesn't have a reason to be angry," Athena said.

"Anywaaaaay," Sierra said, "stop pouting and drink your hot chocolate."

After gliding my fingers across my laptop keys, the screen lit up with my recent search.

Potential jobs for someone who doesn't know what she wants to do with her life.

Sun gazed at my screen, then arched her brow at Athena, who sat across from me. Athena snapped my laptop closed and swiped it off the table, stuffing it into her backpack. I wanted to pout some more, but they didn't let me.

Which, I mean ... was what friends were for, right?

"What?" I asked.

"You're trying to make yourself feel bad," Sierra said.

"No, I'm not."

"Yes, you are," Sun said.

"I'm just trying to find a job, so—"

"You should just be Hector's sugar baby," Athena said, wiggling her brows. "If your dad wants to be annoyed at you for being in love with Hector, then you could really milk it. Let Hector shower you with goodies and fuckings."

"Fuckings?" Sun repeated, giggling behind her hand.

"Tons of fuckings," Athena said.

"I don't think that's a good idea," I admitted.

"Sure it is!" Sierra exclaimed. "Even in the contract you have with him, you're technically his full-time submissive, sooooooo ..." She clapped her hands together and grinned wickedly at me. "You deserve it."

I blew out a breath. "You know what I need? To pee."

And to get the hell away from this table for a couple of moments. They all meant well, but I wanted to run a business too

... *I think.* It felt like such a waste; I would feel like such a disappointment, only being a trophy girlfriend.

Wouldn't I?

My chest tightened, and I scurried down the hallway toward the restrooms, Hector on my mind. What would I even have to do as a full-time submissive? Clean and cook for him? I didn't want to be a housewife, and he loved cooking.

Once I made it to the restroom and did my business, I washed my hands and then splashed some cold water on my face. Maybe it wouldn't be so bad. Hector honestly didn't seem like he would mind.

But how could I even bring that up to him?

Once I patted my face dry with a paper towel, I dumped it into the garbage and stepped into the hallway. I headed back toward my table, but stopped before I could turn the corner, the sound of a man's voice drifting through my ears.

And not just any man. My father.

I tiptoed to the corner and glanced around it to see Dad and Evelyn sitting on a sofa and chatting quietly.

Evelyn's brows were furrowed, and she gripped Dad's hand gently. "It's going to be okay, Jacob. I promise."

"I should have seen it coming," Dad said. "I should have protected her."

"Protected her from who?" Evelyn asked. "Hector? You've seen how sweet he is with her."

Dad's shoulders jerked forward, the way mine did when I cried. "I just thought I knew her so well, Evelyn. But she's been keeping this secret from me. How could I have missed it? Am I such a shitty father that I drove her to this?"

Evelyn squeezed his hand tighter. "You're not a bad father, but you are hard on her."

"So, is this my fault?" he asked, voice cracking.

My chest tightened, and I leaned against the wall, tears in my eyes. I forced myself to turn around and head in the opposite direction because I didn't know what I would say to him if he saw me. I didn't know how he would react.

He blamed himself, and part of me blamed him too. I'd been seeking approval from him my entire life, and when Hector gave it to me … I took it. But at the same time, there was nothing to blame my father for. I'd met the man who I loved the most.

CHAPTER
FIFTY-TWO

HECTOR

THE NEXT NIGHT, I sat on the couch, scrolling through collars on my laptop.

Heather lingered in the kitchen and wiped the already-clean counter with a dry rag, trying to busy herself.

I arched a brow, closed my laptop, and set it on the coffee table in the living room. "What's wrong?"

"Oh, nothing."

"Heather," I hummed, "what's wrong?"

She chewed on her inner cheek and looked over at me. "Can we talk?"

"Come here." I beckoned her over. "What's going on?"

After setting down the rag, she walked over to me and toyed with the ends of her sleeves, which I had only seen her do a handful of times when she was nervous. Instead of sitting down beside me, she stayed standing.

"I wanted to—"

"Sit down," I ordered. "Relax and tell me what's wrong."

"Nothing's wrong." She sat beside me. "I wanted to talk to you about our contract."

I stiffened and briefly glanced back at the laptop, where I had been scrolling through collars that I would like to see fastened around Heather's neck soon. I didn't know when would be appropriate, especially with the drama involving Jacob, but I didn't want to wait.

"What is it?" I asked, sitting up taller. "Did I do something that upset you?"

"No."

When she didn't continue, I pushed. "Do you want to talk about your limits?"

"No," she whispered, grabbing a pillow and holding it to her chest, as if to protect herself and to put even more space between us. "I want to talk about the term *full-time submissive*. Is that okay?"

After turning my entire body toward her, I gave her my full attention. "Yes, that's okay."

"When we entered into the contract and our relationship, you said that it was to become a full-time submissive, which I haven't been for you yet." She paused and swallowed. "I was talking to my friends, and I ... wanted to ask if ... that was still on the table."

"You being my full-time submissive?" I clarified. "Yes."

"What would it entail?" she asked quietly, completely unlike her.

"I wouldn't require much more from you than what you give me now," I said. "Preferably, you would live with me. I would provide everything you need or want in return for you being mine whenever I need or want you."

She opened and closed her mouth a handful of times, but didn't say anything, then averted her gaze. I grabbed the pillow from her and pulled her into my lap, taking her chin so she would look at me.

"What would happen if I had a job?" she asked.

"I would prefer that you didn't have one," I said honestly.

For me, that would defeat the purpose of full-time.

"Really?" she asked. "It's okay if I don't have a job at all?"

"I'll provide everything you need and want," I repeated. "No need for you to work."

"But won't you think less of me if I don't have a job?" she asked, still chewing on her inner cheek and shifting in my lap. "At that point, I would be like a stay-at-home girlfriend, wouldn't I?"

"You still have ambitions, and you can still have goals that you want to work on to better yourself." I pushed some hair out of her face. "You don't have to give up on those. You're welcome to pursue your passions still. Being full-time with me doesn't make me think any less of you. You're giving me something in return."

"What, my pussy?" she said with a small giggle.

"No. Your submission," I said. "Is this something you want?"

"Yes."

My eyes widened slightly because I almost hadn't expected that to come from her. She had always been so set on working with Jacob to impress him, and while their bond had been broken, I'd expected her to dive even harder into it.

"I don't want to work for my dad anymore," she whispered. "I want to find something I want to do with my life, but I don't know where to start. I want to try being full-time with you, but only if that's something that you want—"

"I do," I said, too excited to wait for her to finish. "I want you to be full-time with me."

A smile fluttered across her face, and warmth filled my chest.

"Really?"

"Yes."

"Can I still be a brat?"

I playfully rolled my eyes at her, but wrapped my arms around her body and pulled her closer to me. "As long as you're with me, you can be anything, Heather."

HEATHER

THE EARLY MORNING sun flooded in through the windows of my apartment and cast a glow on the stacks of moving boxes in the corner of my room. I grabbed another empty box and set it on my bed, packing away some items inside it.

After Hector and I had chatted about me officially becoming his full-time submissive—even though I contractually already was—he had asked me to move in with him. While I would continue to pay my half of the rent here and would be back to check in on Sierra all the time, I'd decided that if I was going to try this out, then I was going all in with it.

"Heather!" Sierra shouted from the other room. "Hector is here!"

A couple of moments later, someone knocked on my door as a courtesy. Then, the door opened slightly, and Hector gazed in with a smile and playful eyes.

He walked into the room and shut the door behind himself. "Already packing up?"

"I told you that I'm committing myself to this whole full-time submissive thing."

"Thing? *Relationship,*" he corrected. "Use your words."

My lips curled into a small smile, and I nodded to a couple of stuffed toys that I'd had since childhood. "Can you pass me that thing over there so I can pack it away?" I asked, taunting him with a smirk.

"What thing?" he asked, brow arched and tone sharpening.

"That thing." I nodded to the shelf. "On the shelf."

Hector picked up an empty picture frame that I had been meaning to fill with a picture of us inside it—even though we had no pictures yet together—and held it toward me. "Oh, do you mean this thing?"

"No, the other thing," I said, crossing my arms. "Up there."

After setting down the frame, he grabbed up a souvenir I had picked up on my family's last trip to Maui a couple of years ago. "Do you mean this thing?" he hummed, taunting me back and stalking closer to me.

"No, the stuffed animals," I said, frustrated.

Hector set the souvenir on my desk and grasped my chin in his hand. "Good girl. Using your words for once." A low chuckle escaped his throat as he gently stroked his thumb across my cheek. "Expanding your vocabulary."

I glared up at him. "Excuse me, but I have an extensive vocabulary."

A smirk crossed his face, and he pressed his bulge against my stomach. "I think that mouth is only good for one thing," he murmured, his breath warm in my ear. "And it's not speaking with the extensive vocabulary that you think you have."

Warmth spread through my core, and I pressed my thighs together. "What is it for then?"

While I expected him to shove me down onto my knees and tell me that it was only good for sucking his cock, he twirled me around and bent me over the bed. Before I had much of a chance to react, he was crawling up onto the bed, straddling my hips in prone-bone style.

He placed both hands on the bed beside my head, grinding his cock against my ass. "Whimpering," he grunted lowly into my ear. "Trying to bite back moans when I fuck you in a public space with other people around."

Hector snaked his arm around my waist and sank his hand into my pants, fingers rubbing against my clit. I curled my fingers into the bedsheets and furrowed my brows, the pressure already rising higher inside me.

I curled my toes and moaned into the mattress, but Hector grabbed a fistful of my hair and pulled my head back. So Sierra wouldn't hear me moaning with the door closed in my bedroom, I bit my lip.

"Just like that," he murmured. "Always so embarrassed to feel good."

"I'm not embarrassed."

He moved his fingers faster against my clit. "Then, moan for me."

While I wanted to do nothing more than to moan, I found myself pressing my lips together and not making a single sound. He moved his fingers faster, pushing me higher, and gently sucked on the crook of my neck.

"Has the brat finally been tamed?"

"No, but—*fuuuuuck!*"

A low moan escaped my throat as he flicked my clit with the tip of his finger. I threw my head back, eyes rolling and body seizing underneath him. I pressed my mouth against the mattress and screamed out in pleasure.

Sierra had definitely heard that.

"For a brat, you're awfully quiet today," he taunted. "Let's change that."

Again, he pulled back on my hair so I couldn't moan into the mattress anymore and brought me to the brink of an orgasm again. I arched my back hard, my legs shaking uncontrollably.

"Who's my good girl?" he murmured.

"Hector …" I whispered.

"Who's my good girl?" he repeated.

"Is this all you have—"

He sank his fingers lower and pushed them into my pussy. I whimpered as softly as I could, but when he found my G-spot, I couldn't handle it anymore. He massaged it in small circles, the pressure unbearable, then drew his nose up the column of my neck.

"If you're trying to make me moan, you're going to have to do better than—"

He moved his fingers in a come-hither motion quicker, and I lost it, screaming to the high heavens—a place that I didn't even believe in—for him to stop because the pleasure was all too much. And yet this man didn't stop until I was a crying, trembling mess in his hands.

When he finally pulled his fingers out of me, he stuffed them into my mouth. "Welcome to your first day as my full-time submissive, Heather." His lips curled into a smirk. "I'm going to love having my fun with you."

CHAPTER
FIFTY-FOUR

HEATHER

I TWIRLED my spaghetti around on my fork and gazed out of the foggy restaurant windows into Market Square in the heart of Pittsburgh. Outside the window, snow blew through the breeze. Christmas lights twinkled all around the city for Christmas Eve tonight.

After sucking the strings of spaghetti into my mouth, I gazed across the table at Mom. Soft, flickering candlelight danced across her face as she spoke to Hector, who sat next to me. I still hadn't stopped thinking about the conversation that I'd eavesdropped on at Carnegie Coffee.

Children with their parents giggled and walked through the square, going to and from the ice-skating rink that the city had set up a couple of streets over. I frowned at one father-and-daughter duo, holding hands and smiling widely.

I had absolutely no reason to feel this shitty. I had been the one to betray my father, and people had it way, way worse than I did in regard to their families. Hell, Sierra's entire family had died before Christmas a few years ago. Hector didn't have a family either.

And here I was, complaining that I had disappointed mine. I should be thankful.

"Heather?" Hector asked to my right.

Once I snapped out of my daze, I placed my fork down and wiped my mouth with a napkin. "Sorry, I was just thinking." I set the napkin back down and attempted to clear my mind, glancing at him. "What is it?"

"Are you okay?" Mom asked.

"Yes," I lied. "I'm fine."

"What's wrong?" Hector pushed.

I narrowed my eyes at him, sending him my most menacing glare, then frowned. "Actually, I saw Dad the other day at the coffee shop. I overheard his conversation with Evelyn. And ..." *I'm not sure if I should call him or not. It is the holidays after all ...*

Mom's expression softened, and she reached across the table to squeeze my hand.

"Do you think that I should call him tomorrow for Christmas?" I whispered.

What if he didn't answer? Would this really be my first Christmas without him? I'd texted him so many times the day after it happened, but he didn't return any of my messages, so I stopped trying.

But I couldn't shake the feeling that I'd caused him this pain, which was so stupid because I had apologized over and over again. Yet ... he had walked in on me literally sucking off his best friend and business partner.

On the other hand, how would he react when Evelyn's father found out that he was sleeping with her? I would bet that their relationship was a secret. All of this was so messy and only became messier by the day.

Hector traced soothing circles on my hand with his thumb. "It's your decision, Heather."

Mom offered me a smile. "Your father can be a grinch sometimes. I would know. But I think he'd really like that. If you're ready, maybe giving him a call could be a step in a positive direction for you."

I nodded, still unsure if he would actually answer, and turned back to the restaurant window. I didn't know why he couldn't be the bigger person, why it had to be me, even after I had messaged him endless times already.

My stomach tightened into knots. What would he think when he found out that I was now Hector's full-time submissive? Surely, that would make matters even worse, and I didn't have the energy to deal with that right now.

"Heather," Mom interjected, "your father loves you. You know that, right?"

"Yeah, well, it doesn't feel like it," I mumbled to myself. "But I know."

Soft Christmas music played through the restaurant, the ambience of Christmastime just making me feel all types of ways, some good and some bad. This was the first Christmas that I would spend with a boyfriend … and I couldn't wait to wake up next to Hector tomorrow.

I didn't want the thought of calling Dad to dampen my mood.

After sipping my wine, I placed down the glass. "I'll think about it, Mom."

Mom's smile widened. "That's all I ask, dear."

Once I finished my wine and spaghetti, I set down my fork and nudged Hector. "I'm going to use the restroom before we go home." I scooted past him as Mom excused herself, too, and walked with me to the women's room.

"So, you've moved in with Hector?" Mom asked on our way.

My lips curled into a small smile. "Only for a bit."

"I hope that you're doing okay," she said, slipping into a stall.

I walked into the one beside her and locked it. "Honestly, it's the best."

Better than I could have ever imagined. Better than any other relationship I had been in. There was no competing, no fighting, no accusing or blaming or not feeling like I was good enough. I usually avoided relationships, but I loved being in one with Hector.

"I can see how much he cares about you, and one day, your father will too."

After finishing my business, I washed my hands in the sink and gazed in the mirror at Mom stepping out of her stall. She walked to the sinks and let the water rush onto her hands. Warmth filled my chest.

Nodding, I grabbed a towel and wiped off my hands. "He does, but I know that he's struggling with how to help me through this whole thing. I'm sure you already know that he's never had a father figure, so he doesn't fully understand. Sometimes, I wonder if all this drama is too much for him, you know?"

"Nonsense," Mom said. "That doesn't mean he doesn't know basic human decency. He's a very intelligent man, Heather. He's worked extremely hard in business, and he must've worked through a lot emotionally, growing up in that kind of environment."

I nodded.

"I know that this is probably weird for you," I said. "But you know the terms of my relationship with Hector. I don't know what I want to do with my life, even after all these years in undergrad and grad school. I'm going to finish up this year in grad school and be a submissive for Hector full-time until I figure it all out." With every word I said, my voice became more strained.

I didn't want her to be disappointed in me, too, for this decision. I needed her support, needed her to say that it was okay, because this was actually beginning to feel like something I'd wanted for a long time.

"What do you think?" I asked hesitantly.

Mom smiled at me through the mirror. "I think it's a great idea."

My eyes widened. "Really?"

"Yes, of course."

"You're not ... mad?"

She laughed and dried her hands. "Why would I be mad at you? It's your life, Heather. You don't owe me anything, and you don't owe your father anything either. We both want you to be happy."

Lips quivering, I wrapped my arms around her and pulled her closer to me. She hugged me back the way she used to when I was just a little girl. A hug that I had craved for so, so, so long.

I closed my eyes as a weight lifted off my shoulders. "Thank you."

HEATHER

SPIT ROLLED down my chin and onto my bare tits. I pressed my thighs together around the vibrating saddle that Hector had strapped me to this morning and sucked the ball gag into my mouth, whining against it.

"Hector," I cried, my voice muffled.

Tinsel bounded my arms together behind my back. I had been moving my shoulders back and forth in an attempt to escape since he'd tied me up as a Christmas morning present, but the binds had only gotten tighter, and the bells that Hector had attached to the nipple clamps chimed with even the slightest of moves.

I whined some more in hopes to get his attention, but he sat on the couch across from me, sipping on a coffee mug and scrolling on his phone. By the way his cock bulged in his pants, I *knew* that he was enjoying every moment of this.

"Hector," I whimpered, more spit drooling all over my tits. "Please ..."

Light flooded in from the large floor-to-ceiling windows, soft snow drifting down from the gray sky. Tears welled up in my eyes because I didn't know if I could take any more orgasms this morning. I had completely lost count of how many it had been so far.

Finally, he set his phone down, took one last sip from his mug, and walked over to me.

"You're so pretty when you cry," he murmured, swiping his thumb across my cheek to wipe away a couple of tears. He moved his hand down to grip my chin and tilted it up by a few centimeters. "Look at you."

When he finally unbuckled the ball gag from around my head, he shoved four fingers into my mouth and down my throat. I choked on them and stared up at him through teary eyes, another orgasm ripping through me.

"There you go," he murmured. "How does that feel?"

"Good," I sputtered around his fingers. "So good!"

"Have you enjoyed your Christmas present?"

"Yes," I cried. "Please, I don't think I can handle another—"

He tapped a button on the saddle, and it began vibrating even faster.

"Oh my God!" I screamed, my eyes rolling back into my head. As my legs shook my entire body, the bells on my nipple clamps rang over the soft Christmas music that Hector had playing throughout the penthouse. "Fuuuuuck!"

After letting me ride out another orgasm for a few more minutes, he finally crouched in front of me. Once he stopped the saddle, I fell forward into him and whimpered out in defeat. Hector scooped me up into his arms, walked over to the couch, and deposited me on the cushions. I lay back and took a deep breath, expecting him to release the tinsel binds.

But instead, he crawled between my legs and kissed down my thighs.

"Hector, I-I can't take any more," I whispered.

"Yes, you can." He hovered his mouth over my cunt. "My girl can take more."

Warmth spread through my core from him merely calling me *his girl*, and I spread my legs a couple of inches wider. Hector fastened his mouth between my pussy lips and sucked my clit between his lips.

I arched my back hard and dug my heels into the couch cushion, trying to push myself backward because my clit was so swollen. But as he swiped his tongue across it, I screamed out in pleasure.

"Fuck, Hector," I moaned. "Don't stop!"

"You're being such a good girl for me this morning," he purred.

Which, not going to lie, kinda pissed me off because I didn't like being a good girl.

So, I smacked my lips closed and pushed my heels back into the couch to scooch away from him. He wrapped his arms around my thighs, laid his hands flat on my stomach, and secured me to the couch so I couldn't move.

"Don't start now," he warned.

"You're not going to—"

"If you say one more word, I'm going to strap you back onto the saddle and will leave you there until dinner," he threatened. "Five more hours of constant coming, and your pussy will be too sore to move. So, choose your next words carefully, *brat*."

I bit my lip to stop myself from saying anything stupid and stared down at him, feeling his warm breath against my cunt. He stared up at me through those hard, dark eyes, warning me to keep quiet.

"Don't stop," I whispered.

It took everything in me to say those words instead of something bratty, but I couldn't be fastened to that vibrating death trap anymore today. My pussy was so sore that I could barely move myself now.

A smile traveled across his lips, and I let him have this small victory. He let a wad of spit drip down onto my clit, but instead of rubbing it in with his fingers, he crawled up the couch until the head of his cock pressed against my entrance.

My pussy tightened, and I curled my toes. He shoved himself

into me until every last inch was inside my cunt. Then, he stilled, balls deep. I clenched and unclenched around him, just the way I knew he liked until he finally groaned and pulled out.

His mouth found my nipple clamp, and he tugged up on it, sending pleasure coursing through my body. I curled my toes, loving how quickly he thrust in and out of me. Whimpering, I arched my back harder. Hector sucked more of my tit into his mouth, leaving hickeys all over my skin.

"More," I whined. "Please, I want more!"

Hector slammed faster and harder into me, his breath ragged on my chest. Pressure rose up inside me again, and I exploded all over him, becoming a desperate, crying, whining mess for my Master.

When he finally slowed down to a stop, he rested his forehead against mine and placed a kiss on my nose. "Merry Christmas, sweetheart."

Warmth exploded through my chest, and a giddy feeling shot up and down my body. "Merry Christmas."

CHAPTER
FIFTY-SIX

HEATHER

"SO ..." I hummed, tucking my phone into my purse, standing next to Sierra, and sipping on champagne after Christmas dinner. I told myself that I wasn't going to worry about Dad, but he hadn't texted me yet, and I was disappointed. "How was your day?"

Sierra drew her finger across the rim of her glass and bit back a grin. "Good."

I arched my brow. "Just good? Steven didn't ask you anything?"

On the ride over, Hector had mentioned that Steven was planning on asking Sierra something important today. But I wasn't sure if Sierra knew about it yet, and I didn't want to ruin any surprises.

"No ..." She looked at me, confused. "What would he ask me?"

Stiffening because I *definitely* ruined the surprise, I grabbed her hand and led her across the room toward the leather couch. If I didn't come up with an excuse or go into further detail, she'd definitely continue to ask me all night.

"Hector said maybe Steven would …"

After sitting next to me, she furrowed her brows. "Would what?"

"Give you a contract."

"A contract for what?" Sierra asked.

I scratched my forehead with my red-and-white manicured nails. "To be his submissive."

She stared at me quizzically.

Sierra had definitely seen and read the contract that I had with Hector, so I didn't know why she looked so confused. She and Steven might've started their relationship a bit after ours, but they were very close. I had expected they were officially Dom and sub. Hell, Steven had even given her a necklace as a collar!

I peered over at Hector, who chatted with his brother and frowned. He still hadn't given me one yet.

"Usually, in a BDSM relationship, you have a contract that clearly and legally outlines the boundaries of the dynamic," I explained. "Apparently, Steven had asked Hector for advice about contracts, which isn't something he's done before."

Sierra's lips curled into a frown. "Oh."

I sipped my champagne. "Maybe he's saving it for another day."

"Or another girl," Sierra whispered.

"Excuse me?" I asked, completely surprised and pissed that she would even suggest that. "You'd better take that back, Sea. We both know that man is head over fucking heels for you. Don't you even *think* that there is another girl in the picture."

She laid her head back against the couch and stared behind herself through the window. "I know, but …"

"But nothing," I said, crossing my arms. "If that ever happened, you know I would be the first one to"—I made a snipping motion with my index and middle fingers—"chop off his … precious penis."

A giggle bubbled up past her lips. "I know."

"He's just waiting," I reassured.

"But for what?"

"Maybe he prefers … something else and isn't sure if you're ready for it," I suggested.

Though I wasn't completely sure. This world was so new to me, but there were some things that I realized Hector enjoyed more than others, kinks that I would've never explored without his guidance.

She chewed on the inside of her cheek. "What else could he be into? He's relatively open with me, at least about sex."

I moved closer to her on the couch and gently nudged her shoulder with mine. "I know you've wanted a family since what happened a few years ago, but don't be so hard on yourself. I don't even know Steven, but he seems really happy with you."

She frowned. "What can it be? What do I need to fix about myself?"

"Nothing!" I exclaimed way too loudly that I caught every-one's attention. After recovering by throwing Steven, Hector, and Michelle a small smile, I cleared my throat and lowered my voice. "You don't have to change anything about yourself. He might just be into … something different. And there's nothing wrong with you both learning what you're into."

Tears welled in Sierra's eyes. "I don't want to be with anyone but him. What do you think he's into?"

After shrugging, I looped my arm around hers and rested my head on her shoulder. "I don't know. You should talk to him about it. Hector is into some more punishment and discipline kind of stuff. It could be something darker that Steven hasn't shown you yet."

Sierra chewed on the inside of her cheek and caught Steven peering at her from the table with his siblings. Once she shot him a small smile, she glanced down at her lap, desperately trying to hold back a frown.

"Stop getting into your own head about this," I said.

"I'm not," she reassured.

"You totally are."

Gulping, she turned back to Steven, who waltzed over this way. "I'm not."

"Are you okay, love?" Steven asked, sitting next to her on the couch, his arm curling around her shoulders and his worried gaze on her. "You look like you're about to get sick or cry, or … *both* right now."

My lips curled into a small smile because I was so happy that she'd finally found someone who cared deeply for her, and I excused myself to give them some privacy. I'd just had to open my big mouth and say something when I really shouldn't have.

Phone buzzing in my purse, I yanked it out halfway to meet Hector in the kitchen to see a text from nobody other than … Mom.

Mom: Hope you're having a good dinner!

I frowned and rechecked my messages from Dad to see all the ones I had sent him a couple of days ago. Nothing else, not even possible text bubbles to dance around the screen. I placed the phone back down and looked up at Hector, who smiled softly at me.

He knew that I had been waiting for my father to text or call me, but he hadn't pushed me to drop it or to text my dad. He had spent all day with me, distracting me from the thought, and I didn't think I could ever be more grateful than how I felt right now.

To me, it didn't matter whether or not he had collared me yet. I was taking it day by day and slowly realizing that maybe being a full-time submissive for him wasn't a bad idea.

CHAPTER
FIFTY-SEVEN

HECTOR

HALF DRUNK OFF CHAMPAGNE, Heather swayed on her seat next to me in the dining room. I had given her all the orgasms that she could possibly need this morning as a gift, but I wanted to give her one more gift tonight.

I leaned toward her. "Want to head out?"

"I'm sleepy," she mumbled, nodding and closing her eyes, phone in hand.

She had been checking it throughout the night, waiting for Jacob to text or call her. And I really wished that man would. If he didn't by the end of the night, then there would be another fight at work on Monday.

That asshole had two hours left.

"I'll get your coat."

I stood and headed toward the coat closet. After grabbing my coat, I shrugged it on and draped Heather's over my forearm, catching Steven in the kitchen.

I stretched out my arm. "Merry Christmas."

Once he shook my hand, I helped Heather into her jacket and took her hand. While Sierra napped on the couch, Steven walked us to the door with his hands in his pockets and a disappointed look on his face.

"You did good this year with dinner. Would've made Mom proud," I said, glancing behind him at Sierra on the couch. "I know it's been hard on you since she passed. She was the only real person we all had. But now, you have Sierra."

After following my gaze, he smiled softly and nodded. "Yeah, but ..."

"But?"

"I didn't give her the contract," Steven said, clearly upset.

He had asked me for advice on contracts this past week and told me that he planned to give Sierra a BDSM contract, the first one he had ever presented to a submissive. But, God, I knew how nerve-racking that first contract was.

"Hey," I said, squeezing his shoulder. "You have time. Don't rush it."

"I should've," he said, shaking his head. "She gave me a present that ... meant more to me than any other present someone had given me before. And I chickened out on gifting her a simple contract."

"It's not just a simple contract," I said, releasing his shoulder and giving him a small smile. "My first time was hard too. There's a lot of trust you both have to put in each other. Don't get down on yourself. It'll happen."

Heather swayed beside me, and I decided that there was no way that she'd make it to the car like this.

So, I picked her up and tossed her over my shoulder. "I have to get this one home. Just don't wait too long, Steven. Don't want her thinking that you're using her. That's the worst that can happen."

After he said goodbye, he shut the door behind us. I carried Heather to the elevator, and when we reached the bottom floor, I walked with her through the lobby and to my car. We didn't have a far distance to travel, but it was cold outside today.

As I opened the car door, she shifted in my arms and stared up at me through sleepy eyes. "Are we going home?" she murmured.

"Yes," I whispered. "Can I wake you when we get back? I have one last surprise for you."

She widened her eyes slightly. "You do?"

Warmth spread through my chest. "I do."

"Wake me up," she said, closing her eyes again and relaxing in my arms. "I love your surprises."

FIFTY-EIGHT

HEATHER

"HEATHER, WE'RE HOME." Hector nudged gently.

I slowly blinked my eyes open to see the doors opening on the elevator to Hector's penthouse. After shifting in his arms, I jumped down to my feet and held on to his elbow for balance. My eyes were so heavy, but I really wanted to be awake for his present.

He had mentioned that he had one more for me, and because this was our first Christmas together and because I'd had the best time of my life despite Dad being an absolute dick, I didn't want to ruin our day because of my brattiness. I didn't care how much I wanted to crawl up into the bed and have his big arms envelop me.

As I walked into the room, the lights turned on throughout the living room. I wandered to the large floor-to-ceiling windows and stared into the dark night. More snow had fallen, blanketing the city, and the holiday lights twinkled in the distance.

Warmth spread through my chest as I glanced over my shoulder at Hector.

"I had the best day today," I whispered with a smile.

After leaning toward me, Hector placed his mouth on mine and let his lips linger on our kiss. "This has been my favorite Christmas in a long, long time." He cupped my face. "But it's not over yet."

"Technically, it is," I hummed, rocking back on my heels. "It's 12:01."

"Technically ..." he dragged out. "You'd better get your ass on that couch before I toss you."

"Sounds fun." I giggled and turned around to head to the couch because I didn't want to be annoying to him right now.

We'd had our fun this morning, and it seemed like Hector really wanted me to be good.

When I jumped up onto the couch, Hector disappeared into the other room. I toyed with a knitted red blanket that Hector used as a throw on the couch and tugged it around my shoulders, waiting in anticipation.

A couple of moments later, Hector walked out from the hallway with a black gift box.

My eyes widened, and I chewed on the inside of my cheek. I didn't know what it was, but I was beyond excited. I hadn't felt this excited for a gift since I had been a child. While Christmas morning had come and gone, this felt more like it than anything.

"So," I said, "what is it?"

He set it on my lap. "You'll have to open it to find out, but first"—he grabbed one of my ankles and undid the strap of my heel—"let's get you out of these." Once he undid the other and pulled them both off me, he nodded and sat next to me. "Okay."

While Hector was the most confident man I knew, there was something about him, sitting underneath the twinkling Christmas lights, that made him so vulnerable right now. I clutched the box in my hand and leaned in to kiss him again.

Because I honestly didn't care what was in the box. I'd love anything from him.

"I love you," I whispered.

"If you love me, I think you'll love what's in the box more."

My lips curled into a smirk. "I doubt that."

I opened the box and pulled out the black tissue paper, revealing nothing other than a thick black collar that read the words *Hector's Brat*. My eyes widened, and I looked between him and the collar several times.

"This is ... this is for me?" I said, voice barely above a whisper. "Really?"

"Of course it's for you, Heather," Hector said. "Do you like it?"

"Hector ..."

Tears welled in my eyes, and I tried to form a response—I really did—but so many emotions were rushing through me right now. My fingers were shaking, and all I could think about was ... how much he really loved me.

Hector tucked some hair behind my ear. "Heather, are you okay?"

I burst out into a fit of tears and sobbed loudly, burying my face into his chest and hugging him tightly. I didn't know what to say, and I didn't think something like this would ever mean so much to me.

But with Dad not even messaging me today, I ... I felt some type of way.

A way that I didn't think I would be able to fix, to heal, to fill.

After placing the box and collar on the coffee table, Hector wrapped his arms around me and pulled me closer to him, his warm breath on my hair. "If you don't like it, I can get you a new one. We don't have to—"

"I love it," I cried, pushing away tears with the back of my wrist. "I'm sorry. I'm a mess."

He gently released me from his hold and smiled. "You're not a mess."

My lips twitched into a frown. "I don't deserve you."

"Don't say that." Hector captured my chin in his hand and lifted it so I'd meet his gaze. "Understand?"

"Yes."

Though I was still getting used to loving myself despite what everyone else thought of me. It was hard and terrifying, but I knew that it'd be so freeing. One day, I would have to face Dad and tell him that I was Hector's full-time submissive, and I'd have to be okay with that.

"Pull your hair back," Hector said, taking the collar from the box.

My heart raced, and I pulled my hair up so he could fasten it around my neck. Gently, he wrapped it around my throat and buckled it in the back. Then, he drew his fingers against the letters, and his smile widened.

"You're mine now," he said.

I bit down on my lower lip to suppress a small giggle. "Good."

Just as he was about to lean in for a kiss, a sudden bang on the front door echoed through the penthouse. Hector's soft expression hardened, and he got up from the couch and walked to the door.

It was after midnight. Who the hell was—

When he opened the door, a tall man in a police uniform stood in the doorway. "Hector Patton?"

"Yes, that's me," Hector said, brows furrowed. "What's going on?"

"We received a call regarding a break-in at your office earlier this evening. The office is locked up, but the alarm has been set off," he said, arms crossed over his chest. "How would you like us to proceed?"

FIFTY-NINE

HECTOR

"I CAN'T BELIEVE I let you talk me into allowing you to come," I said, hand gripping the steering wheel.

Heather sat in the passenger seat, wrapped in her knitted blanket and staring out the windshield. Somehow, she had weaseled her way into the car after I told the officer that I'd come check it out.

Jacob hadn't answered his phone the three times I called him on our way over. *Prick.* And of fucking course, this had to happen literally moments after I gave Heather her collar. She'd had such a huge smile on her face, and I had been so happy.

There goes that.

"I wasn't going to let you come alone," she said. "What if something happens?"

"Exactly why I should've come alone."

If something happened to her, I would fucking lose it.

"Well, I'd rather be here with you than pacing around our home and wondering what the heck was happening," she said, furrowing her brows even harder and crossing her arms. "So, take that."

While I wanted to stay mad at her, she had just called the penthouse *our* home, and it made me feel some type of way. So, I stayed silent and pulled into an empty parking spot in front of our office building. The officer pulled behind me.

Heather unbuckled her seat belt.

"You're staying in the car," I said.

"But—"

"Heather," I growled even more sternly, taking her chin in my hand. "Stay here."

Streetlights cast shadows on the empty sidewalk. I unbuckled my seat belt and gave Heather my most stern look. I didn't want to ever hold the collar over her head, but she needed to behave. This was for her own safety.

"I'm your Master, and it's my job to keep you safe. So, I don't care how hard you pout; you're not coming in with me. I don't know who's in there or what the fuck is going on. You're lucky that you're in the car. Stay."

Heather's expression fell, and then she nodded. "Okay, I'm sorry."

Once I kissed her on the lips to show her that I wasn't mad, I exited the car and walked to the office building with a couple of officers. I entered my key code, and the door clicked open. One officer nodded to me.

"You can stay here," he said. "We'll check it out."

"No, I'm coming in with you."

After they peered at each other, he nodded. I followed them into the building and headed straight for the elevators. They swept around the first floor, but if someone was going to steal anything, they'd head up to the top.

Though I had a feeling that it wasn't a robber at all.

Up and up and up, the elevator whizzed to the top floor in seconds. When the door dinged and opened, a strong scent of booze drifted into the lift. I blew out a low breath and closed my eyes.

Fuck.

Once I gathered up enough of a shit, I stepped out into the main office and spotted Jacob sprawled out on one of the couches, his hair disheveled and a distant, sad look in his eyes. He clutched a bottle of tequila.

"It was you who tripped the alarm?" I asked, walking farther into the room.

Jacob gazed up from the couch, staring through me. "Yeah."

"Why didn't you turn it off? Or answer your phone?"

Instead of answering me, Jacob took another sip right from the bottle. "How was Christmas with my daughter? Did you get her everything that she could ever want? She deserves it."

"She deserved a fucking call from you," I growled. "It's Christmas."

"I didn't think she'd want to talk to me," he whispered emptily.

I snatched the bottle from him and recapped it. Then, I threw it into the trash so he couldn't get any more hammered tonight. I wondered where Evelyn was. Surely, they had spent today together, too, hadn't they?

"She has been waiting impatiently by her phone all day," I said. "For you."

Eyes glazed over in a drunken gaze, he shook his head. "I'm a bad father. I wasn't there enough while she was growing up. I was too hard on her. She always told me that I was being too hard. I drove her to you."

Who is *she?* His ex-wife maybe?

Tears welled in his eyes, and a sob escaped his throat. "I should've called her."

"You should've."

Usually, I wasn't one to add insult to injury, but he deserved it. Yet my words only tore him into even sharper pieces. He dropped his shoulders forward and sobbed into his hands, shaking his head.

I sighed and sat next to him, deciding that insulting him wouldn't get us anywhere. "I can't imagine how difficult this must be for you. I know that it has been tearing Heather up since you found out about us."

"Tell her I'm sorry," he sobbed, wobbling back and forth on the couch and still crying way more than I had ever thought he could. He started mumbling incoherently, but I made out the sentence, "I should have handled things differently."

After running my hand over my face, I stood up and wrapped my arm around his to lift him to his feet. "It looks like it has been a long night, Jacob. Let's get you home, and you can talk to Heather when you're sober."

Though I wasn't sure how I was going to get him home with Heather in the car, nor did I know how Heather was going to react when I walked out of the office with him. But I couldn't let him rot here.

Not if I wanted him to respect me as Heather's ... boyfriend.

And hopefully, one day, something more than that.

CHAPTER
SIXTY

"WHAT'S TAKING HIM SO LONG?" I muttered under my breath.

With the knitted blanket sprawled over my shoulders, I'd had my gaze locked on to the entrance of the building since Hector had disappeared inside it fifteen minutes ago. My worry grew with every passing minute, and I couldn't help but think of the absolute worst.

What if my professor had come to enact revenge?

I chewed on the inside of my cheek, my knees bouncing. If something happened to Hector because of me, I would never forgive myself. The police were in there with him, but what if they couldn't stop it?

So, without hesitation, I grabbed the door handle. I needed to at least see …

Just as I was about to open the door, my phone buzzed on the center console. I snatched it quickly to check if it was Hector, only to see a message from Evelyn appear on the screen.

Evelyn: Is your dad with you???

Evelyn: I've been messaging him all night! He said he would

be gone for about an hour, but that was three hours ago! And he's not answering his phonee. I think something happnned to him.

Evelyn: pls answer.

The more messages that came through, the less and less they were legible. She was truly worried about him.

Me: Sorry, I don't know where he is.

Me: I haven't talked to him in a while. He didn't call me today.

Wow, I sounded like a bitch, but it was just the truth.

I chewed on the inside of my cheek and glanced back to the office doors, eyes growing wide. Maybe ... Dad had actually come down here to check on the alarm, and someone had gotten to him. Maybe someone had hurt him.

After thrusting the door open, I jumped out of the car and tossed my blanket into the back seat. Hector might not want me to come in there, but if Dad was in here and something happened to the both of them ...

Just as I hopped onto the sidewalk, the doors opened. My jaw slackened as Hector had one arm around Dad's shoulders, and Dad was stumbling out of the building with the support of his enemy/business partner.

"Oh my God! What happened?!" I exclaimed. "Was someone—"

"Jacob broke in," Hector said. "He's drunk."

"I'm not drunk," Dad slurred, lifting his head. "I'm sad that—"

When his gaze landed on me, he stopped his sentence short and stared at me through drunken, sad eyes. I furrowed my brows, so confused and heartbroken and then even more confused because why the hell was he here of all places, getting drunk?

"Dad, what are you—"

"I'm sorry, Heather," he slurred, leaning toward me, but Hector held him steady and away from me. "I-I'm so sorry ... I didn't think … I wasn't sure. I should've called you. I've been thinking about you all day, and I'm such a bad daaaaa …"

I stared at him, tears pricking my eyes. "It's okay, Dad."

Hector glared at him like it wasn't okay.

"You should get home," I said to him, stepping forward and gently placing my hand on his shoulder. "Evelyn just messaged me and said that she's worried about you. Why didn't you tell her that you were coming down here?"

"I'm sorry," Dad continued to slur. "I've been such a bad dad to you."

"We need to get him home, Heather," Hector said.

After nodding, I opened the back door. Hector helped him into the car, and Dad rested his head against the headrest. I headed around to the other side and hopped into the passenger seat, adjusting the rearview mirror to see him.

"I'm sorry, Heather," Dad said, shutting his eyes. "I'm so sorry."

CHAPTER
SIXTY-ONE

CHEWING on the inside of my cheek, I glanced into the guest room. Dad slept on top of all the blankets, his mouth half open and snoring as loud as I remembered from when I had lived with him and Mom. But somehow, it was nostalgic.

After I had searched everywhere for Dad's keys and couldn't find them, we'd brought him back to Hector's penthouse and patiently waited for Evelyn to come pick him up. She was about an hour outside of the city with her family for Christmas. But she was worried about him.

So, here we were, waiting up at nearly two in the morning for her.

Hector gently placed a hand on my shoulder and squeezed. "You okay?"

My lips quivered. Once I shut the door so I wouldn't wake Dad, I turned around and wrapped my arms around Hector's waist, burying my head into the center of his chest and sniffling softly. "I'm okay, I think."

To be honest, it had been such a long night that I didn't know if I would be okay in the morning. All I knew was that I was so fucking thankful that I had Hector with me. And not only that, but he … had given me a collar tonight.

Which had made my Christmas so, so good.

"How are you feeling?" Hector asked, grabbing my hand and leading me to the bedroom.

"I don't know."

Eyes heavy, I sat down on the edge of the bed and leaned back on my hands. I wanted to pass out, but I wanted to be here when Evelyn arrived to make sure that she was awake enough to drive him back home.

"You need to sleep," Hector said, pulling down the blankets. "You've had a long day."

"But—"

"Get to bed, Heather."

"Hector, I need to be here when Evelyn—"

"What you need is sleep," Hector said. "Now, get in bed."

I sighed through my nose and crawled up the mattress and underneath the blankets to please him. But I didn't have any plans to actually fall asleep until she got here. Dad and I really needed to talk, and I couldn't if he got into a car accident and died.

Especially after Sierra's Christmas tragedy a few years ago, I wasn't taking any chances.

Hector drew his hand over my hair, petting my head softly. "You did great today."

My eyes widened slightly, a warm feeling rushing through my body. "I did?"

It wasn't often a brat like me received praise, but I might've … sorta liked it.

"So amazing," Hector continued, his soft touch making me relax on the pillows. "I'm so proud of you for the way you reacted when you saw your father. I thought you were going to start bawling, and I would have to toss him onto the sidewalk and bring you home."

A giggle left my lips, and I closed my eyes. "You would not."

"Ah, you say that now, but I was ready to hit him if he said anything to you."

"Thank you," I whispered, a small smile crossing my lips as sleep began to take me. "Thank you for everything, for today, for tonight, for the collar you gave me. I never thought I could mean so much to someone."

He placed a soft kiss on my forehead. "You mean everything to me, Heather. I love you."

SIXTY-TWO

HECTOR

AFTER THE ELEVATOR doors opened on Monday morning, I stepped out onto our floor, sipped my coffee, and headed straight for Jacob's office. Evelyn nervously glanced at me from her desk, but I continued without saying a word to her.

Once I gave a soft knock, I opened the door and peered into the room. "Have a minute?"

Jacob nodded and stood, gesturing for me to sit across from him.

I hadn't talked to Jacob since Heather had passed out the other night and Evelyn had come to pick him up from my guest room. But today, Jacob was sober and quieter than usual, something obviously on his mind.

Heather had mentioned that he asked her out for dinner tonight, but I needed to talk to him before then, in case he tried to talk shit to her about our relationship or about me. He wasn't going to ruin the only good thing in my life.

"I'd like to talk about Heather," I said, sitting down in front of him and making direct, firm eye contact so he would know that I wasn't going to back down. We were going to talk like adults without any fists being thrown or fingers being broken.

Jacob cleared his desk, turned off his computer, and flipped over his phone so there weren't any distractions between us. Then, he cleared his throat and sat up straight. "Before we start, I want to apologize for the other night."

"For what exactly?"

"I shouldn't have been here, drinking my life away," he said. "That was wrong of me."

Did Evelyn knock some sense into him yesterday?

"It would've made us as a company look bad if anyone found out about that," I hummed. "Just don't do anything like that again. And if you plan to, do it somewhere that isn't our office. You scared the fucking hell out of Heather."

"How's she doing?" Jacob asked. "Good, I hope."

"She's good," I said. "You'll see her tonight, right?"

"Yes."

"And ... if you don't mind me asking, what're you going to talk to her about?"

"I asked her to dinner to apologize," Jacob said. "Nothing more."

I pressed my lips together and narrowed my eyes at him, waiting for him to break, waiting for him to stumble all over his words, which would tell me that this was all a lie and that he planned to do more than just that over dinner.

But his expression stayed neutral.

"I don't care if she's your daughter anymore," I warned, feeling more protective over her than any other woman—or any other submissive—I had ever had. "If you hurt her, it's not going to go over well between us."

"I'm not going to hurt her," Jacob said. Then, a couple of quiet moments passed, and his expression softened to a smile. "You love her, don't you?"

"Yes." I stood. "And I will do what I can to protect her. Even from her own father."

CHAPTER
SIXTY-THREE

HEATHER

I SAT in an upscale Italian restaurant in the heart of Pittsburgh across from Dad and twisted my fork around the pasta on my plate. My stomach had been in knots since I had sat down because I didn't know what to say to him. I didn't think I needed to say anything.

While I completely understood that no father wanted to see their daughter sucking off his business partner, I had apologized multiple times and felt terrible about it. There was nothing else for me to say to him.

"So"—Dad cleared his throat—"how was your Christmas?"

"Good," I whispered.

Another long pause fell over the table, and Dad shifted uncomfortably.

"How was yours?" I asked, my heart stinging from the anticipation of him telling me how wonderful life was with Evelyn. And I mean, I was beyond happy for him, but I ... I just wished that he would apologize to me too.

Dad grabbed his glass of whiskey and sipped. "Terrible."

After snapping my gaze up to him, I widened my eyes. "Terrible?"

"Spending time with Evelyn was great," Dad clarified. "But I … I missed you."

My lips quivered, and I dropped my gaze back down to my food so he wouldn't see the tears in my eyes. I didn't want to show him how much he'd hurt me because he was hurt too. And talking about our feelings together was never really our thing.

"I missed you too," I whispered so softly that I almost didn't hear myself.

"You did?" he asked in disbelief.

Gaze flickering back up to him, I nodded. "Yes."

He stared back at me with a plethora of emotions crossing his face, and then he finally settled on a frown and sad, desperate eyes. "I'm sorry that I didn't call you or make an effort to see you yesterday. I … I haven't been able to stop thinking about how I failed you."

"You didn't fail me," I said. "Maybe pressured me a lot, but you didn't fail me."

"But, Heather …"

"Stop it, Dad. It's weird, especially now that you're dating someone my age. What does her father think about you two? Does he think he failed her?" I asked, realizing quickly that maybe her dad didn't even know about them yet. "Even if he doesn't know, how do you feel about her because I know it's more than you hooking up with her? You're happier."

Dad looked at me for a long time in silence, then dropped his gaze. "It's hard."

"What's hard?" I asked. "Being with Evelyn? Because that looks easy for you. I saw how you were with her the other day at the coffee shop."

"He's my business partner," Dad said. "And you're my daughter. It's hard, Heather."

"Well," I whispered, "it's not going to get any easier for you."

As the words tumbled out of my mouth, I realized how harsh

they'd sounded, but I meant every single last word. I didn't want to apologize to him anymore about my feelings toward Hector.

We shouldn't have kept it a secret, sure.

But I loved him.

Way more than anyone else.

"I have—" I started.

"I'm sor—" Dad started at the same time.

After smacking my lips together, I glanced across the table at Dad and stayed quiet. I never thought that those words would leave his mouth, never mind ever being said to me for how he'd acted. But maybe he was apologizing for something else …

"I'm sorry for the way that I treated you and for the way you felt like you needed to go behind my back," Dad said, avoiding eye contact with me because, again, feelings were not our forte with each other. "You're an adult and allowed to make your own decisions about who you date and spend your time with. I'm sorry."

I pressed my lips together and nodded. "I forgive you."

Dad snapped his gaze up to mine and furrowed his brows. "You do?"

"Yes, but I'm not going to stop seeing Hector," I said, sitting up a bit taller and finally feeling a bit more confident in who I truly was. "I love him, and we're in more than just a contractual relationship with each other."

"I understand," Dad said, a small smile creeping onto his face.

"And also …" I paused, unsure if I *should* continue. "There's something else."

Dad's smile tightened, and a strained laugh left his mouth. "Please, don't tell me that you're pregnant."

A giggle bubbled up past my lips, and I shook my head. "No, I'm not pregnant. We're smarter than that." Although we never wore any protection, but he didn't need to know that. "I've decided that I'm not going to work with you anymore. It's not what I want to do, and I know that you've wanted me to, especially if Aaron isn't going to one day run the company. But it's not going to happen, and I don't want ..."

When I realized that I was just rambling away, I sucked in a breath and stared back at him. It was a bad habit that I had tried to get rid of since I'd left high school, but it always came back when defending myself in front of him.

"Okay," Dad said. "That's fine."

My eyes widened. "You're not mad?"

"Why would I be mad?"

"Because I thought that ..."

Dad arched a brow. "That I'd be mad at you for not wanting to do what I do?"

"Yes," I squeaked, feeling like a mouse.

"I've come to realize that I don't care what you do with your life, Heather. I just want you to be happy. And from what I can tell, Hector makes you happier than you used to be. So, I'm okay with whatever you decide to do with your life."

"Are you sure?" I asked.

"Yes." He paused. "Why?"

"Because ... right now ..." *I'm kinda just Hector's whore.* "I'm just trying to figure it all out."

Dad smiled at me. "That's okay."

"Okay ..."

We fell into another silence, but this time, it wasn't as awkward as the first few.

Dad smiled at me from across the table, and I smiled back, finally feeling like I had him back in my corner again.

SIXTY-FOUR

HEATHER

"SO?" I hummed, leaning back against the balcony that overlooked Pittsburgh and gazing at my bestie. I pulled my white fur coat over my shoulders, my fingers grazing against the collar around my neck, and placed one of my red-bottomed shoes against the concrete wall. "Did you give him the contract back?"

"I want to do it when the time is right," Sierra said, looking into the restaurant's double doors at the New Year's Eve party, her gaze on Steven.

Apparently, he had given her a contract to officially be his submissive. And it was about time!

Steven and Hector chatted with each other over a glass of wine on the suede white couches as Athena stumbled onto the balcony after flirting *heavily* with Charlie, who leaned against the bar, his hazy gaze never once leaving her.

"You sure the contract looks good?" Sierra asked.

Athena threw her arm around Sierra's shoulders. "You literally haven't given it back to him yet?!"

I threw my arms into the air. "That's what I'm saying."

"The contract is perfection." Athena giggled, some of her

shimmering orange hair falling into her face. "I honestly don't think that a contract could be more in your favor. You can step away and cancel it whenever you'd like."

With a drink in his hand, Steven approached the double doors that led off onto the balcony.

"Professor Big Dick is here," I hummed, pushing myself off the balcony and grabbing Athena's hand to drag her stumbling ass back into the restaurant. "Have fun out here!" I shouted to Sierra. "Make sure to give him a big ole smooch at midnight!"

When we made it back into the restaurant and bar area, Athena slipped away to Charlie, and I found my way to Hector, who stood from the white couch.

"Look at this," Hector said, handing me his phone.

I sipped on my drink and stared down at the news article. The headline read, *Professor Arrested for Blackmailing Grad Students*, and the image accompanying it was of Professor Eric in handcuffs.

"Serves him right," I said, handing the phone back and smiling.

"Thoroughly deserved."

My brow arched at how calm Hector looked. "Did you have something to do with this?"

"Maybe." His lips curled into a smirk, and he glanced behind me, his gaze distancing. "Look."

Twisting around, I searched the crowd and spotted Sun with a husband and wife that I vaguely recognized from Radiant. Sun's cheeks were flaming red, and she shuffled from foot to foot, glancing at the wife through her lashes.

"Are they ..." I started.

"A thing?" Hector finished. "I don't know."

A giggle slipped past my lips. "I hope so. Sun needs some. She's too innocent."

"If she's with them"—Hector chuckled—"she's not innocent. She's—"

"Sweetheart!" someone called from behind Hector.

I shifted back and spotted Mom walking toward us with a

man about her age a couple feet behind her. I had never seen him before, but Christmas Eve, Mom had mentioned that she had been seeing someone new.

"Sweetheart, this is Tyrell. Tyrell, this is my daughter, Heather."

After shaking his hand and greeting him, I waggled my brows at Mom, who smirked at me, then at him. I arched a brow, wondering what that was all about when I noticed that *he* actually looked embarrassed. Or maybe he was nervous.

"Heather, you're here," Dad said from behind me.

With Evelyn's hand in his, Dad walked up to our small group, his gaze traveling to Mom. They greeted each other, but didn't introduce their partners to each other. I chewed on the inside of my cheek and inched closer to Hector.

Awkward!

Well, sorta.

While Mom and Dad had been very okay with their divorce, I couldn't remember a time where they both had someone new on their arms to introduce to the other. And with the way Dad had treated me over Christmas, I knew Mom was still angry with him.

"Well, we ought to get going," Mom said, saying goodbye and leading Tyrell away.

"You're okay with Tyrell?" I asked Dad when Mom and Tyrell disappeared through the crowd.

"Why wouldn't I be? I'm not going to let her Dom me again."

"What?" I asked.

His cheeks reddened, and he grabbed Evelyn's hand and headed through the crowd, glancing back at me with a small, embarrassed smile. "Enjoy New Year's! We'll catch up this week, Hector."

When he disappeared completely, I scrunched my nose. I did *not* want to hear about my parents' sex lives, and I really had *not* expected that Mom would've ever been a Dom to Dad. My head felt like it was going to explode.

"Ew," I said.

Hector chuckled again. "Ah, now, you know what I've known for years."

"You knew about that?!"

"That's how I met your mother and father. She was Domming him at Radiant."

"Gross!" I exclaimed. "I do NOT want the details!"

Suddenly, the countdown to midnight began all around us. After looping two fingers around my collar's circular ring, he drew me closer until our lips were millimeters apart. Warmth exploded between us, and I curled my fingers around the flaps of his suit jacket.

And as everyone shouted, "One," Hector gently cupped my face in his large hands and drew me closer to him. His lips crashed down onto mine, and I smiled against him.

Who knew that I'd wrap this year up by kissing my father's best friend?

Join Emilia's newsletter to read the epilogue

ALSO BY EMILIA ROSE

Stepbrother

Poison

The Bad Boy

Detention

My Brother's Best Friend

Science Project

Excite Me

Mafia Boss

Mafia Toy

Sex Education

Pornstar

Submitting to the Alpha

Come Here, Kitten

My Werewolf Professor

The Twins

My Bad Boy Alpha

Summoning Sex Demons

The Breeding Cave

Next Door Incubus

ABOUT THE AUTHOR

Emilia Rose is a USA Today bestselling author of steamy romance. She loves writing about dirty-talking bad boys who are obsessed with innocent, and sometimes insecure, virgin heroines. She currently lives in a small town in Connecticut USA with her husband and three playful cats.